WALLS

OF

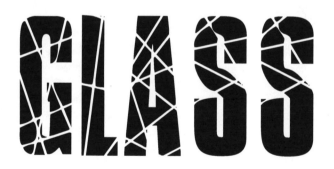

GLASS

J.W. ELLIOT

Bent Bow
Publishing

Bent Bow Publishing
P.O. Box 1426
Middleboro, MA 02346

ISBN-13: 978-1-7336757-7-2

Cover Design by Brandi Doane McCann

If you enjoy this book, please consider leaving an honest review on Amazon and sharing on your social media sites.

Please sign up for my newsletter where you can get a free short story and more free content at: **www.jwelliot.com**

Internal art work:
Pen sketches by Conrad D. Ruiz
Walls of Glass image by diki_pinwheel

TO ALL THOSE WHO SUFFER FROM
DISCRIMINATION OF ANY KIND.
MAY YOUR BURDEN BE LIGHTENED.

WALLS OF GLASS

CHAPTER ONE
THE PLAGUE OF A POOCH

I blame it on the dog. He came out of nowhere, trailing a cloud of red dust. He zipped past the third baseman and launched himself through the air. I was halfway to first base before I realized he had caught my beautifully-placed fly ball. The only thing I could think was, does that count as an out? I ran through first base just in case, choking on the rust-colored dust that turned my sweat to red glue.

A rattle of laughter came from the bleachers as the shortstop and left fielder chased the stupid dog around. I walked back to first base and stood there like a dope, trying to decide if I should run to second or wait for them to tear the ball from the dog's mouth. One coach waved me over and pointed to the bleachers.

"Take a seat," he said from around a cheek full of tobacco.

I dropped onto an open space on the bleachers behind the dugouts and scowled. I thought I'd done a good job reading how the pitcher always followed his fastball with a slider. I was the first kid to get on base for a while. That should count for something—even if a mangy old black and white dog tried to eat my fly ball.

I glanced around at the mixture of white, black, and Hispanic boys bursting with energy and eager to strut their stuff. The lanky black kid I sat next to stared at me with an expression that said he wanted to squash me like a bug. Two other black kids turned around to glare at me, and I realized I had made a big mistake.

Apparently, scrawny white boys weren't supposed to sit next to the black kids. I hesitated for just a second, unsure what I was supposed to do, until the lanky black kid jerked his thumb to tell me to get out of there. I acted like I remembered something important and hurried away to sit by a fat white kid. My backside barely touched the bench before he shoved me off. I hit the dirt with a grunt.

"Place is saved," he said.

The Stillwater Oklahoma Welcoming Committee must have forgotten to send out the memo about "love thy neighbor as thyself." I gave up with the kids and went over by the adults who clustered around the coaches because I figured the adults, at least, would be civilized. One guy with a big belly and a clipboard spit tobacco juice on my shoe and called me "boy." He actually spit on my shoe. What kind of jerk does that?

I wiped the spittle off in the dirt, but I just created a long red streak. Some kids whispered behind their hands and snickered when someone pointed at my sneakers. A group of them laughed. Well, my sneakers were old and getting thin, but I had a nice tear in one that let the air blow through so my foot didn't get so hot. All the other boys had cleats. I tried to act like I didn't notice their sneers. I was new and only twelve years old. What else could I do?

The scruffy old dog padded around panting and dripping slobber on everyone he could reach. He nosed right up to me like he thought I might be nice to him since he caught my ball. I could see the coaches looking at me sideways, so I shoved the dog away. I didn't want them thinking it was my dog and disqualify me because the pooch had been running around the ball field getting in the way.

When they called me to the field again, the stupid dog followed me out. I kicked dirt at him and had to wrestle him for the grounder that came my way. I got it, but the kid kept running and made it to third base before I could chuck the ball to home to stop him. That didn't seem too fair since they pulled me out when the dog caught my ball. Some adult stalked out and collared the dog, dragged him off the field, and tied him to a post.

Every time a ball came my way that dog set to howling like a cat was chewing on his tail. He started up again as a grounder bounced toward me. I caught it in my glove and chucked it to first base, but the dog kept howling.

"Shut up," I yelled, and everybody turned as one to stare at me.

By the time they ran us through our paces, I had developed a terrible urge to slap that shaggy mutt on the nose for ruining my tryouts. I dropped on the wooden bleachers, boiling in my own sweat, while they called the A team and the B team and the C team. My name was the last one called for the D team.

The boys filed off to their respective teams while I sat and watched them go. Most of those D team kids couldn't even hit the ball, let alone catch one, and all the black kids were placed on the C and D teams no matter how good they were. I watched the entire tryout, and I knew for a fact that a lot of those black kids played better than most of the white kids on the A and B teams. But what did I know?

The dog knocked over a trash can and poked his nose into the mess. He trailed a frayed piece of rope he must have chewed through. I glared at the dog. It was his fault. He raised his head to look at me, and I snatched up a dirt clod and chucked it at him. The punk dog caught it in his mouth and wagged his tail like he thought I wanted to play.

My brother, Clint, had been right. No new kid would catch a break—especially not one harassed by a dirty old flop-eared dog. It's not like I expected to be on the A team, but the D team was downright insulting. Kicking a dirt clod with my air-conditioned shoe, I stuffed my glove under my arm and slid my hands into my pockets. My head bent under the sweltering Oklahoma heat, I shuffled off toward home.

"Didn't I say you'd be wasting your time?" Clint said from behind the new *Star Wars: The Empire Strikes Back* comic book. He reclined on a pile of boxes in our bedroom.

It was the summer of 1980, and *Star Wars* fever was running high. My experience at the ballpark showed me that galactic battles raged in more places than the movie theaters. I wiped the red dirt from my baseball glove and oiled it before dropping it back

3

into its box. The lingering smell of oiled leather gave me a pang of regret. I loved baseball and that wretched, stinking dog had ruined it all for me.

"No new kid was gonna get on a decent team," Clint said. He lowered the comic book to his lap. "This isn't Idaho."

Thick, brown hair fell in front of his eyes. His jeans had holes in the knees that let his pale, white skin show through. He was cool and a lot smarter than me.

"They put you on the worst team, didn't they?"

I grunted. Last year, my Little League team had been undefeated. I played left field, and I could chuck a ball all the way to home plate from the outfield fence, but I didn't want to talk about it.

Clint gave me a knowing look, so I escaped back outside into the purgatory of heat. I couldn't lounge in front of the air conditioner where Clint would rub my nose in my failure. The earth shimmered as the heat waves rolled over me. Even the insects complained. They buzzed and whined. The grass struggled to grow, and the streets in town were paved with cement because asphalt would have melted.

Idaho may not have been the Garden of Eden, but Oklahoma sure felt like Hades. No matter how many clothes you stripped off, the only cool place in the entire state was right in front of the air conditioner or maybe a swimming pool, but we didn't have one of those.

Why did we have to move 1,300 miles to a house filled with mice? A house with yellowed grass in the front lawn, and nothing but dirt and bugs in the back? The grass crunched underfoot as I headed for the cement road. The heat burned right through the bottom of my sneakers. Even the wind breathed hot against my face.

I moped all the way to the shabby little park at the end of the street and sat on a swing that hung from rusty chains, wishing yet again that we could go back to Idaho. At least I had friends there. Here, I had stepped into an alien universe where even the bugs played by different rules.

I wasn't going to complain out loud. Dad went to school so he could get a better job, and Mom worked full-time to keep food on our table and a roof over our heads. Still, making friends wasn't easy.

It always happened the same way. The new kid showed up in a town where all the kids had known each other since they were getting their diapers changed, and he was supposed to squeeze right into all that history. These kids had been playing together, going to school together, fighting with each other, and, in some cases, kissing each other, for years. There was nothing they didn't know about one another. Just saying "hi" to someone could drop you smack dab in the middle of a civil war that had been raging from the time they were slobbering on the same toys in pre-school.

As the new kid, the only sensible thing to do was to keep your head down and your mouth shut until you figured out who the local Darth Vader was and where Obi-Wan Kenobi hung his jacket. Once you had that worked out, you could try to find the normal kids that inhabited the star systems in between—preferably closer to Obi-Wan. That wasn't so easy either, because all those normal kids had been watching the galactic battles raging for twelve years. They learned to mind their own business and to be wary of strangers. How did they know I wasn't some psychopath sent to draw them to the Dark Side?

It took a while before people even noticed you were alive. Then it was another month or two before you could talk to each other because no one wanted to be the first one to break the ice. I tried that once after our last move to Idaho, and I got punched in the mouth for it. I knew all this, and I went to the baseball tryouts anyway.

I squinted up at the raging sun that tried to bake me where I sat swinging back and forth on the creaky swing set. It got warm in Idaho, but nothing like this. I don't know if the earth came closer to the sun in Oklahoma or what, but the sun down here could be downright dangerous. I thought my brain would boil.

Something warm and wet touched my hand. I jerked with a shriek and flopped from the swing into the dirt. I expected some monster Oklahoma bug to be crawling up my arm. Instead, a soggy baseball dropped on my stomach and rolled to the ground. The mangy dog panted over me. How had he found me? And why did he still have a baseball? Didn't this dog have an owner?

"Get out of here," I shouted.

The dog bounded away and crouched low with his tail wagging.

He barked. I grabbed up the slimy ball he had dropped and sprang to my feet. I chucked it away. The dog raced after it.

I ran out onto a rickety bridge that spanned a creek with steep cutaway banks to find a place to hide from the dog. The creek sliced through the park to disappear into a tangle of willows and brush that lined its banks. I leaned on the rails and peered down at the sorry excuse for a stream. The floor of the creek was muddy with a trickle of water slithering through it like a snake that was too hot to move.

I scrambled down the muddy bank and stood at the edge. The creek smelled like an old garbage can with a rotten cat tossed in. If the temperature hadn't dropped by at least twenty degrees in the shade, I might have left. For that kind of relief, I could endure the stench of a dead cat for a while—at least until the dog left me alone.

Creeks have a way of accumulating the leftover trash of the lives they pass through. I found stuff down there that must have washed up from the nineteenth century—boots that could have been worn by General Custer, bottles, shopping carts, bags of trash, dead opossums, and the biggest snapping turtles I had ever seen.

I nearly stepped on one the size of a car tire. My whole leg could have fit into its mouth. He glared at me with beady black eyes like he wanted to eat me. He snapped his beak, and I jumped halfway out of my skin, putting some real distance between me and the monster turtle. I wasn't used to this kind of stuff.

The turtles in Idaho were cute and tiny. You could take them home and make pets out of them. I gave that monster turtle all the room he wanted and kept walking. Maybe the snapper would eat the dog if he came down here after me. That was when I saw the wallet shoved up under the edge of a rock and half-covered in mud.

CHAPTER TWO
THE WALLET OF DESTINY

Man, what a wallet!

It lay half-open, inviting me to pick it up. Dozens of green bills bulged from the pocket. I shoved the rock aside and snatched the wallet from the stinking mud. The stack of bills packed inside that thing could have fed my family for months—maybe years. I looked around, in case the owner was looking for it, but I couldn't see anyone.

I peeled the soggy pocket open. When I pulled on the paper driver's license, it ripped. The mushy paper tore free and fell into the mud. I picked up the pieces and tried to see who owned the wallet, but the ink was so smudged from the water or stained by the mud, all I could read was the name—Damon. The paper crumbled.

Maybe I should have left the license alone and dried the wallet first, but it was too late now. A bark rang up the creek. I glanced up to see the dog staring down at me. He picked up the ball he had set on the bridge.

"Jeez, what's wrong with you?" I shouted. "Get out of here."

He dropped the ball into the creek and barked again. I strode over, picked it up, and threw it as hard and as far as I could. The dog took off with his claws scraping over the wooden bridge. I thought I heard a bang and a crash, but I was too distracted by the wallet.

7

I stuffed the wallet and the pieces of the license into my pocket and scurried for home before that dumb dog could find me again. All the way there, I tried to convince myself that this Damon guy didn't need all that cash or he wouldn't have lost it. This wasn't any different than me picking up a twenty dollar bill I found blowing around in the gutter, was it?

My family could use the money. Dad was working a part-time job while he tried to get a doctorate degree. Mom worked herself ragged trying to raise a family with six kids while still holding down a full-time job. Life was hard for my parents. I wanted to buy a new trumpet for band so I didn't have to play one of those dented pieces of metal I rented from the school. They all sounded more like an elephant with asthma than a trumpet. Mom needed new shoes for work. I could think of a million things to buy with all that cash.

I was still reeling from the apparent good luck of finding a soggy wallet packed with bills when I got home. Things like that just never happened to me. I locked myself in the bathroom and pulled out the lump of waterlogged bills to count them. They were cold and damp and still had the rich, dizzying smell of new money, despite the moldy stink they picked up in the creek. Ben Franklin stared right up at me like he was congratulating me on the first good luck I'd ever had.

Damon had three thousand twenty-six dollars in his wallet! I had never seen that much money in one place before in my life. Maybe I could buy a silver Ford Mustang! The look and smell of that stack of green bills were making me crazy.

Only after I counted and recounted the bills did I bother to look for more identification. I hoped I wouldn't find any because by now that money had cast its spell on me. Everything was so wet and stuck together that I couldn't salvage much. There was a picture of a white guy in a suit with a bow tie and another one of a chubby, dark-skinned baby girl with a pink bow in her hair.

Damon had a tiny picture of a football team, but there was no other identification. I tried to piece together the driver's license again, but the paper had crumbled even more in my pocket. There hadn't been a photo on the license, which told me it was old. My dad had come home just yesterday with his new license and told us that photos were now mandatory in Oklahoma. He passed his license around so we could all make jokes about how he looked like a criminal without his glasses.

I sat on the toilet lid with the bills and the pictures spread out on the sink trying to decide what I should do. I knew what I *should* do, but did I *want* to do it? I decided to ask Mom.

Someone banged on the bathroom door, and I jumped.

"Dude, are you growing roots?" my big brother yelled. "Other people need to use the bathroom."

He tended to exaggerate when it came to bathroom time. I hadn't been in here more than a few minutes. Arguing with him would only cause trouble though, and right now, I didn't need any more of that. I stuffed the wallet into my pocket and yanked the door open just as he prepared to pound again.

"About time," he said and pushed past me.

Mom scurried around in the kitchen getting dinner ready. I had been smart enough to wash my hands and clean the mud off my clothes so she wouldn't suspect I had been places I shouldn't be. She smiled at me.

"How did the tryouts go?"

I shrugged. "I'm not playing."

She cocked her head in surprise. "But you love baseball."

"Not if they're gonna stick me on the D team with all the goof-ups who don't even know which end of the bat to hold."

She gave me that oh-you-poor-thing look.

Mom had six children. After all those kids, her face might have slipped into a permanent frown. She might have developed that wild and worn out look you often saw on the ladies at the super-market who wrestle their kids away from the candy bars. But she hadn't. Mom was pleasant and quick to smile. Her curly brown hair made her look like a dark-haired version of Shirley Temple.

"When the coaches see how good you are, they'll move you up," she said.

I shook my head.

"Well, maybe next year," she said.

"Yeah," I said, but I wasn't interested in baseball anymore.

A war was raging inside of me. My heart craved that pile of cash. I could still feel the cool, damp bills in my hands. I knew I should tell someone, so I opened my mouth to tell Mom about the wallet, but the wrong words came out.

"Is it wrong to keep money you find lying around in the street?" I dropped my gaze to the floor before Mom could look at me. I didn't want her to see the struggle behind my eyes.

"If you know who it belongs to, you should return it," she said. "But if it was just blowing in the gutter, there's not much you can do." A pot clanged on the stove, and I stole a glance at her. She wasn't looking at me.

"I'm sure you'll do the right thing," she said.

"Okay," I said. But Mom had only made things worse.

If I did the right thing, I wouldn't be able to buy her a new car and new shoes. If I told her now, she would freak out at the sight of all that money and call the police. They might arrest me for stealing the wallet, even though I had only found it. If I turned the money into them, they would just keep it instead of trying to find out who it belonged to. There *had* to be a better way.

I wandered into the front room, clicked on the radio, and dropped onto the couch as *Journey's* song, "Any Way You Want It," burst from the speakers. I stared at the wall, trying to convince myself that three thousand twenty-six wasn't any different than five bucks.

Even the ancient law of "finders keepers, losers weepers" was on my side. By the time the song ended, I had given up the struggle. Though it hurt me more than I can say, I decided to take the wallet back and leave it for a few days to see if the owner would come looking for it. Since I didn't want to risk losing the money, I pulled the bills out and slipped in a note that said "I found your money. If you want it back, call this number."

I rounded the corner before the park and found a black and white police car pulled up in front of the playground. A blue-uniformed policeman stood talking to a bunch of kids by the swings. A brown car with a smashed windshield parked by the curb. The cop wore a pistol on one hip and a billy club on the other. The mangy old dog sat on its haunches beside the police officer with a dirty ball between his paws. I was busted.

CHAPTER THREE
BUSTED

The cops were already looking for me. Somebody must have seen me take the wallet and called the police. I stared at the police officer's gun for just a moment before my twelve-year-old brain betrayed me completely. Instead of walking up to him and explaining what happened, I turned and ran. How did I know somebody from the baseball tryouts wasn't trying to frame me for some crime I didn't commit by sending that dog after me? Maybe the wallet had been planted there just so I would find it and pick it up. No matter what I said, they would accuse me of stealing the money. Who would believe the new kid in town? If I showed them the remains of the driver's license, they would just say I destroyed it so I could claim the money.

I raced back to the house faster than I had ever run around the bases on a ball field, telling myself all the way to calm down. Nobody saw me. They couldn't know I had the wallet. I was just being paranoid. I pounded into our front yard just as Dad pulled into the driveway. He passed a hand over his balding head and jammed a thumb toward the backseat.

"Hop in."

Clint burst through the front door like he had expected Dad, and we clambered into the back seat. My heart still raced a million miles a minute, and I just about tossed the wallet into Dad's lap and blubbered out a confession, but I was too winded and too

11

scared even to do that. I just sat there, slumped down below the window so the cops couldn't see me, and imagined what life on the run from the law would be like.

Maybe if I took the wallet back in the morning, no one would know the difference. I could just sneak out before Mom made us unpack, and I would stuff it back under the rock. If no one came for it after a week or two, I could call the police and tell them I found it. Then they would let me keep the money. Now that I had a plan, I thought I'd be able to relax. But I couldn't. I kept sneaking little peeks out the rear window to see if the police were chasing us.

Since our family had so many kids, we couldn't afford a van or a suburban. We owned a long green station wagon that rumbled down the street like a tank. It wasn't a nice shade of green either. Mom called it lime green, but the rest of us called it puke green. I couldn't help but think the wad of cash I had hidden in my room could have purchased a nicer car for my family.

Dad drove us to the Stillwater newspaper office where we applied to work as paperboys. I guess they needed help in a bad way because we both left with jobs that started the next day. Delivering papers wasn't anything new to me. I had started delivering the morning paper in Buhl when I turned ten years old.

That night, I dreamed a pack of carnivorous turtles was nibbling at my nose and toes. I threw one hundred-dollar bills to scare them away, but they just gobbled them up. Then the monster turtle waddled over, grabbed my whole foot in his mouth, and started to swallow me alive. I woke up to find my brother, Clint, yanking on my foot.

"Get up," he said. "Mom wants these boxes unpacked before the picnic."

I threw my pillow at him, which was a mistake, and I knew better. We had feather pillows that turned hard as a rock if you wadded the feathers up on one end. Clint grabbed up the pillow with a look of pure evil in his eye, shook all the feathers to the end, wrapped the rest around his hand, and slammed it into my head so hard he rattled my teeth. Man, that gave me a major headache.

"Get up," he said as he brandished the feather club. "I'm not doing all this by myself."

WALLS OF GLASS

I raised my hands in surrender. Pillow fights with Clint never went my way. I rolled off the bed and crawled to the boxes. The wallet would have to wait.

Unpacking was worse than packing. Where did we get all that junk? Dad must have had a million books. Mom had at least that much in canned food. And Clint and I lugged all the boxes around and unpacked them. My little brothers and sister were too small to do much but get in the way. Mom and my older sister, Dawn, cleaned the kitchen, making sure everything got put in the right place.

That's when the gray mouse sprang out of a box of peaches.

CHAPTER FOUR
DEATH WISH

The mouse froze in terror for just an instant as it locked eyes with Mom. I didn't know which was more terrified, but I knew which one screamed the loudest.

Mom's shriek rang in my ears. It kept coming and coming. The mouse had to know its days were numbered because it leapt off the box and hit the floor in a long skid that sent it careening into the wall. It scrambled for traction as it whirled and headed for the corner. By this time, Mom was hopping up and down from foot to foot. If she could have pulled it off, she would have clawed her way to the top of the fridge.

I sprang after the mouse, trying to stomp on it, but it was too fast. It hit the corner just before my foot did and headed right back towards Mom. She shrieked louder and louder, each shriek going up in pitch, until I thought my eardrums would explode and the windows would shatter.

Then the mouse scampered right up Mom's pant leg. I thought she might faint or die or something. The little lump squirmed up her pant leg while she jumped up and down, screaming bloody murder. I guess the mouse figured since it had already taken the plunge, it might as well get in as deep as it could. But Mom wasn't having it. She got a murderous look on her face. She slammed her hand on the mouse and squeezed. Once she had a hold of him, she didn't let go. She screamed and squeezed and squeezed and screamed.

I stared in shock and disbelief for an entire minute while Mom kept up a little wiggling jig of terror punctuated by a shriek every time the leg with the mouse on it hit the floor. By this time, she had an audience. The entire family had gathered in the kitchen.

"Honey?" Dad spoke real soft and gentle, the way he sometimes did to my little sister.

Mom looked at him with a wild expression, like she had lost her mind.

"Honey?" he said again. "It's probably dead."

Mom glanced down at her hand and stopped dancing. A wet stain was spreading on her pants. She uncurled her fingers from the mouse-sized bulge in her pant leg, sucked in her breath, and looked away. Dad peeled the rumpled cloth away from the wet lump and shook it. Mom gritted her teeth and grabbed the counter. Her knuckles turned white. The smashed mouse plopped onto her shoe and rolled to the ground.

That mouse was pulverized—really pulverized. Guts, teeth, and fur were all mashed together. Dad tried not to smile, but I could see the sides of his mouth twitching. He lifted Mom's hand and led her to a chair like you would someone who was going into shock and then motioned to Dawn to get her a glass of water.

Dawn trembled with suppressed laughter as she set the glass on the table. Clint burst out laughing, and then we all laughed. Dad tried to be sympathetic. I imagine he didn't want to sleep in the doghouse for laughing at his wife, but nobody—and I mean nobody, could have resisted the urge to laugh. Well, nobody but Mom.

The smashed gray mouse so traumatized Mom that we arrived an hour late to the hospital picnic. Like most boys, I could eat just about anything as long as it tasted good, wasn't alive, and didn't have legs. But they had something at that picnic I had never seen before. At first, I thought it was some kind of weird Jell-O with funny looking whipped cream on top. When Mom plopped a big spoonful on my plate, I grew suspicious. It didn't smell right.

Still, being a boy, I took an experimental bite and gagged. Someone had grated carrots into lime Jell-O and spread a thick layer of mayonnaise on top. Mayonnaise! The mixed flavors of lime, carrot, and mayonnaise were never meant to enter the human mouth at the same time.

After spitting that devil's brew into the grass, I escaped to sit with my back to one of the huge trees that looked like it had leprosy. It had smooth, white bark with little, brown patches that peeled off. That's when I saw the bug. I just about dropped my plate. The thing had a green head, bulbous eyes, and wings the size of a hummingbird's. Man, was it ugly!

"It's a cicada," someone said in a high nasal voice.

I glanced up to find a skinny blonde kid standing over me. He held a piece of watermelon in his hand twice as large as his head. His unnaturally clean clothes made me scowl with suspicion. This was not a normal kid.

"What?" I said.

He pointed. "The bug. It's a cicada. They don't bite." He said this like he thought I was some kind of pansy who was afraid of a bug.

I shrugged, hoping he would go away, but Mom approached us with a thin, short-haired woman with a chin as sharp as a knife and dark, dead-looking eyes. I didn't like the look of Mom's new friend. Something about the way she studied me deepened my suspicion. It seemed crafty and calculating.

"This is Mrs. Spencer and her son, Jeremy," Mom said. "They live just around the corner from us." She gestured with her fork toward me. "This is my son, James."

"Why don't you come over tomorrow," Mrs. Spencer said, "and you and Jeremy can play." Mrs. Spencer said this with a sickly sweet grimace, and Jeremy examined me with a new expression—the kind a hungry carnivore might give its prey.

I didn't get back to the creek until later that afternoon. The sun sagged low in the sky as if it had grown tired of trying to boil my brain. The wallet felt like a lump of lead in my pocket, and I just wanted to get rid of it. I didn't want to leave it under the rock right by the bridge where some other snot-nosed kid might find it as easily as I had done.

Still, I needed to do the right thing. I stalked down the creek, sidestepping the monster turtles and winding my way amid the refuse of human lives that lay strewn about the creek. I stomped through the mud a good thirty or forty yards before I saw the crumpled pile of clothes—only it wasn't just clothes.

A man lay curled up as if he had just lain down to sleep by the big log. He twitched. At first, I thought he struggled to stand up—until I noticed the turtles, about a dozen of them. Some were green or brown with yellow spots, and there were several snappers. They all fought to pick at his hands and face. My stomach clenched tight like it wanted to spill my lunch all over the creek.

The sight of those turtles picking at that man's eyes and nibbling on his fingers brought out the coward in me something fierce. I screamed like a banshee and beat it. I didn't know if his ghost was coming after me, but I swear something was chasing me. I knew it. And I didn't stop running until I scrambled back up the bank and stood in the park, covered with mud and panting like I had just sprinted a mile.

Only then did I glance back to see if some monster snapping turtle or disembodied spirit was coming after me. The gully remained silent and undisturbed as if a corpse wasn't lying down there in the mud and trash. It seemed as if a corpse's presence should have drawn someone's attention. The entire city should gather around to find out which of their neighbors had died alone in a nasty creek bottom. The birds continued to cry to one another. The bugs kept on whining, and I knew I had to go back.

I couldn't suppress that ghoulish, horrified interest in things that are dead. How often does a kid get a chance to see a real corpse? I had seen one at a funeral once, but this wasn't the same thing. This was a real live corpse.

When I came up to the guy with my guts all churning and my knees knocking, I found the turtles still picking at him. I chucked a couple of rocks at them, and they scurried away. Now I could see he was a black man with curly gray hair. He looked like he must have been a grandpa, but it was hard to tell.

Something about the way he lay there against that log, as if he had been trying to stay alive, made me feel real sick. I knew I should get the heck out of there and call the police. But I was a scrawny twelve-year-old whose brain had not yet fully developed. I knew it hadn't because my dad always told me that, since my brain was tiny and undeveloped, he would be my frontal lobe until I grew one in my mid-twenties. That was a long way off, so I did what any self-respecting, brain-damaged twelve-year-old would do. I swallowed the bile in my throat, plugged my nose with one hand, and nudged him with my shoe.

"Hey," I said.

He might have been sick or on drugs or something, but he rolled and came back to lying on his side. He was dead all right.

Then, I realized how stupid I had been. How was I going to explain to the police that I hadn't done anything wrong? My footprints were all over the place. Shoot, they might think I killed the guy. And they were probably already looking for me because of the stupid wallet. I couldn't just go home and call them. They would trace the call and match my footprints to my shoes before I could get rid of the wallet. Still, I couldn't leave a dead guy in the creek either.

My mom's words floated through my head: "I'm sure you'll do the right thing." I couldn't let her down.

Before my messed-up brain could change its mind, I ran home, hopped on my bike, and peddled a good two miles from my house to a pay phone booth by the library. I wasn't goofing around. They wouldn't catch me.

I slipped inside the glass booth and regretted my decision. The closed doors muffled the sounds of the traffic outside, but, man, was it hot in that booth. Sweat already dripped from my hair after the bike ride and now it ran down my back and face like a dam had burst. If I stayed in there too long, I would drown in my own sweat. I dropped in a quarter and dialed the police with a quivering finger.

"Stillwater Police. Is this an emergency?" the voice asked.

"Um, not really," I said.

"Please hold."

Jeez. Why do they do that? Just because I said it wasn't an emergency didn't mean it wasn't important. I guess I should have started by saying I found a dead body. That would have grabbed their attention. But I didn't think of that, so I had to wait while I trembled in my shoes and dripped sweat all over the phone. I worried that my quarter might run out.

Another voice came on—a woman's.

"May I help you?"

"Um, I just wanted to report that I just saw a dead body in the creek at Myer's Park."

"A what?"

"A dead body. The turtles were uh—"

"What kind of body?"

That question stumped me for a second. How many kinds of dead bodies existed?

"It's just a body—you know, a guy," I said.

"What's your name?"

"Uh, I want to remain anonymous."

"How old are you?"

"Uh, I just thought you should know."

"What's your address?"

Okay, this was getting serious. If I didn't get off that phone soon, she would get me to spill the beans, and my life would be over.

"Thanks for listening," I blurted. "I think you should go check it out." I slammed the phone down on the receiver.

I banged out of the phone booth, grabbed my bike, and sped away as fast as I could peddle. I'd read enough books to know the police could trace phone calls. I didn't want to be anywhere near that phone booth when they did. Still, I felt a whole lot better. I had done the right thing, just like my mother said.

I found Clint lying on his bed reading comic books. He collected them, so he usually had one in his hands. I escaped to the backyard because I was too nerved up to sit still. Not only had I just called the police about a dead body in the creek, but, on the way home, I realized that I had forgotten to wipe my fingerprints off the phone and to muffle the sound of my voice.

I'd seen enough detective movies to know better, but I was too scared to think of it. I grabbed the rope tied to the tree in our backyard and scrambled up as far as I could get, but I couldn't see the park. Nothing happened. I waited and waited. No police cars came screaming down the road. No flashing lights. Nothing! Man, hadn't they believed me? Did they think it was just a prank phone call?

CHAPTER FIVE
THE TALKING DEAD

knew I should stay away and let the police handle it, but I could feel that man calling to me—like he had attached a line to my brain and kept tugging at it. I tried to resist, but it didn't seem right that he should lie down there all alone, without any friends. Someone should sit with him. Someone should be his friend. In the end, I went to talk to him while I waited for the police to come.

I found him where I had left him. No turtles picked at him now, but I could see something had been at him. The shadows had grown long, and it would be dark soon. The cicadas screamed away. Now and again, a bird brushed through the leaves overhead. No air stirred. Even the wind was too hot to move.

Boy, this guy was in bad shape. His body collapsed in on itself and shriveled up. Flies buzzed around him like he was an intergalactic space station. Bones poked through his clothes. The smell coated the inside of my nose and mouth and made me feel like my stomach wanted to crawl right up my throat. I stood back and covered my face with my hand.

"You don't look so good," I said. "Is there anything I can do for you, while we wait for the police?"

Boy, was that a mistake because at that moment his head rolled so that the empty sockets were staring up at me. His jaw moved like he was trying to say something and a glob of maggots belched

WALLS OF GLASS

from his mouth. I jumped back like I'd just been struck by lightning. I beat it as fast I could slip and skid through the mud and part way up the bank.

Once I was more or less out of range, I studied him—or what was left of him—from the top of the bank. He didn't dress like a bum or a bank robber. He just wore normal clothes. I couldn't look at his face though. It was too gruesome for words. Instead, I just talked in his general direction.

"Man, you scared the crap out of me," I said. "You're dead. You can't go around talking to people when you're dead."

He didn't answer this time.

"I'm sorry, man," I said. "What happened to you? I mean, how did you end up down there? Where's your family? How come you're not home with them now?"

I sat on the bank, picked up a twig, and flipped it through my fingers.

"My name's James—not Jim," I said. "We just moved here, and I don't know anybody. So, I guess that's why I'm here talking to you."

I flipped the twig.

"You must know what it's like not to have any friends. Where are your friends, anyway? Why hasn't anyone come looking for you?"

The cicadas screeched, and the crickets joined in. To my surprise, I realized it didn't matter that this guy couldn't talk. I didn't need him to. I just needed someone to listen. Everyone else was too busy settling in.

"I had friends back in Idaho," I said. "Lots of them. I played football, took Judo classes, and I played on the champion baseball team. I even had a girlfriend. Man, she was pretty. Do you like blondes? Well, she's my best friend's girlfriend now. Does that make sense to you?"

I shook my head.

"It doesn't, does it? Friends aren't supposed to do that kind of thing, are they? You know, it hurt my feelings when he sent me a letter telling me how gorgeous she's getting. But you don't have to worry about that, do you? Have you got a wife? What's her name?"

I glanced down at him. He lay cold, silent, and sagging against the dirty log.

21

"I'm sorry this happened to you," I said. "I called the police, but I don't know if they're gonna come. I'm just a kid. I don't think they believed me."

By now, the aroma of the rotting man was starting to get to me. My stomach kept climbing up my throat, and my eyes rolled around. I guessed I should go see if Dad had come home so I could have him call the police. Maybe they would believe an adult. I jumped to my feet when the sirens howled in the distance.

"I've got to go, man," I said. "Good luck with the police."

I scrambled the rest of the way up the bank into fresh air that was so thick and hot I could almost chew it. It tasted of death and guilt. I sprinted across the road and into the tangle of underbrush behind the houses just as the police cars screamed around the corner. When I got to my house, I clambered over the back fence and snuck in the back door.

Clint stood with his face plastered to the window when I tiptoed unnoticed into the front room. Then he rushed outside. I wanted to follow, but I was afraid to show my face. The police might have hidden a camera in that phone booth. They would find my footprints all over the place. They might think I killed him and be waiting for me to mingle with the crowd, like any respectable criminal. I tried to keep my imagination on its leash, but I couldn't help it. It jerked free and ran wild while I curled up on the couch and trembled.

CHAPTER SIX
A FRIEND FROM THE DARK SIDE

Wash those hands before you play." Jeremy's mom peered down at me with her lip lifted in a sneer.

Well, that's what she said with her mouth, but what she said with her eyes and her expression was quite different. Her gaze swept me from head to foot. Her nose wrinkled in disgust. I understood what she meant to say. "Wash your filthy hands, you vile little boy, before you touch anything in my house."

When I washed my hands at the kitchen sink and reached for the towel, she yanked the towel away and handed me a paper towel. I struggled to figure out what was wrong with the adults around here—first, the fat guy at the baseball tryouts spat on my shoe, and now this woman acted like I deserved to be smashed on the *bottom* of hers.

Monday morning had arrived. Since the police hadn't arrested me yet, I had come to visit pretty-boy Jeremy, as promised. I took the long way around to avoid the yellow police tape that flapped in the breeze all around the park. I didn't have any choice now but to wait a few days before I could take the wallet back to the creek.

Jeremy lived in a one-story house with a fenced-in backyard. I wouldn't call it an ugly house, but it wasn't any mansion, either, though no one would have known it by the way Mrs. Spencer acted. She even made me kick off my shoes when I went in. I saw her eyeballing the hole in my sock where my big toe stuck out.

I almost forgot it all when I saw the intergalactic playground that was Jeremy's room. A huge Millennium Falcon and an Imperial Cruiser rested on his bed with all the action figures laid out around them. An All-Terrain Armored Transport Walker stood beside the bed. *Star Wars* posters plastered his walls. I thought I had been ushered through the pearly gates into heaven itself. The last three years of my life had been spent drooling over this stuff at the toy store. Every part of them was familiar. I reached out a trembling hand to touch the Millennium Falcon. This was the stuff of my dreams.

Jeremy had other ideas. He snatched the Millennium Falcon out of my reach and established our relationship.

"You can play with those," he said, pointing to a pile of toys in the corner. "I get the ships and the Walker."

My gaze followed his pointing finger to a heap of Jawas and two Sand People. That's when I decided I wanted to go home, but I didn't. I fiddled with the Jawas and Sand People while he told me what to do with them. I guess I hoped he might let me handle the Millennium Falcon eventually, but I had misunderstood my purpose there.

When his mom called him for lunch, I thought it was about time. I followed him into the kitchen with my stomach rumbling. But I came up short when I saw only one plate on the table. A huge turkey and tomato sandwich sat there with a side dish of chips and a glass of milk. Jeremy climbed up on the chair and settled into his lunch.

I tried to decide what to do. Back in Idaho when I played at my friends' houses or they played at mine, we always fed each other. I had never had this happen before. What could I do but stand there like a loser?

"You can wait in the front room if you want to," Mrs. Spencer said. "But don't touch anything."

Well, I didn't want to wait, but I had been taught not to be rude. I plopped down on the rust-colored couch and stared at the walls. Jeremy crunched the chips and slurped the milk while my stomach growled like a hungry bear. Once again, I realized I didn't understand the rules that people used down here.

WALLS OF GLASS

My first week I made the acquaintance of a corpse, a brat and his ornery mother, and a no-good, mangy dog. I liked the corpse a lot better than the brat or the dog. At least he was interesting, and he was a good listener. I started having dreams about him, too. Weird dreams that left me shaking and sweating even though the big box fan in the corner of our room blew right on me while I slept.

I dreamed about rushing, churning water, and suffocation. I could hear a voice screaming in terror, but I couldn't hear what it said. The boiling torrent of dirty brown water buried me, rolled me over and over, tore at my clothes, and filled my mouth. Branches clutched at my flesh until the entire world dissolved into darkness and pain.

CHAPTER SEVEN
A LAWBREAKER ON THE LAM

I didn't find out what happened in the park on Saturday night until I came home from Jeremy's house to deliver my Monday afternoon papers. I hadn't gone to put the wallet back because the police taped off the whole area. But the story was front-page news. "Body found in Stillwater Creek," it read.

My hands trembled so much when I tried to read the article I had to lay it on the floor. The story told how a boy made an anonymous phone call that led police to search the creek where they found a decomposing body. No identification had been found on him, and they didn't know who he was.

I stopped reading. No identification meant no wallet. My insides twisted into a horrible knot, and my face burned. I thought I had been scared before, but now my terror paralyzed me as I bent over the paper. Body? Wallet? Holy guacamole!

Maybe *I* had his wallet. I meant to take it back, but then I found the body and called the police. It hadn't occurred to me that the two might be connected, but the police wouldn't be that stupid. If I turned in the wallet now, they would think I robbed the body before calling them. They might even think I killed the man to get his wallet.

Now I was in some deep doo-doo. I must have broken a dozen laws without meaning to. I left my tracks all over the stupid creek bed, and my fingerprints all over the phone booth.

WALLS OF GLASS

The article continued. "The police request that anyone with information about the body or the anonymous phone caller come forward."

Holy crap. Now I was a criminal on the run. A lawbreaker on the lam. A felon fleeing justice. I pinched myself to make sure I hadn't been dropped right into the middle of the *Twilight Zone*. I kept waiting for an alien to appear and tell me I was part of some terrible lab experiment. But it never happened, no matter how much I wished for it.

The little bridge over the creek and the yellow tape that snapped in the breeze drew me like a magnet. The tape sported big black letters that read, "CRIME SCENE DO NOT ENTER." I bicycled past the park two or three times, but I didn't dare go over to the creek. I knew the police would expect me to return to the scene of the crime—at least that's what the criminals always did in the movies. I wanted to go stick the wallet back in the mud and forget the whole thing had ever happened, but I couldn't go down there. Not yet.

I quit haunting the place and rode away to deliver my papers. My paper route ran through the part of town that still had dirt roads and big, overgrown, marshy areas. I flipped my papers onto my customers' porches as I rode. It might sound like bragging, but I could hit a screen door with a newspaper at full speed while dodging under tree branches and bunny-hopping curbs.

When I neared the wild overgrown area where the dirt road cut into the trees, I came across something I had never seen before. I rolled past an old, black lady as big as a boat trying to coax her lawn mower into chewing its way through a jungle of weeds.

Her two big legs planted on the ground like masts on a ship as she leaned into the mower. The loose skirt she wore clung to her sweat-drenched legs. She had tied a big, white bandage around her calf that had a yellow splotch on it with a red center, just like a bull's eye. She favored the leg with the bandage, and I could tell it hurt her.

I considered stopping, but I didn't know her and my last experience with the black kids at the ballpark convinced me I didn't understand how things worked around here. In the end, I just kept peddling. Still, that part of my brain that understood right from wrong eventually won out.

After I finished delivering my papers, I sneaked back to see if she was still there. She was, but she was limping badly now, and she was soaked, like a rain cloud had burst overhead but the rain only fell on her and nowhere else. The yellow-red patch on her leg had grown, too, like a cancer. I dropped my bike in the driveway and walked over to her, not sure how to approach a strange black woman without making another mistake. She saw me coming and let the engine die. I think she was relieved for a chance to take a break.

"I'll mow for you if you want," I said with a shrug.

She looked at me with a sad expression and passed a big hand over her forehead. Sweat cascaded onto the parched grass as she leaned on the lawn mower.

"I can't pay you," she said. She wiped a weary hand over her brow.

"I wasn't looking to get paid," I said. I pointed toward my bike with the paper bag on the handlebars. "I've got a job."

She sighed and smiled. "Would you do that for me, child?"

"Yes ma'am," I said.

"Bless you, son," she said. She hobbled into the house without another word.

The screen door banged behind her as I stepped up to the mower and yanked on the cord. It roared to life. After no more than five minutes, I regretted trying to be nice. This wasn't just mowing a lawn. It was a galactic battle against the Dark Side. I swear ten weeds sprang up for every weed I cut down. They attacked the lawn mower and tried to strangle it. It sputtered and coughed, and I backed out and went at it again. If only I had a lightsaber, I could have made short work of that weedy army of Stormtroopers.

An hour later, I let the lawn mower gasp and sputter to silence as I wheeled it onto the driveway. My sweat dropped on the cement and sizzled. My head swirled. I thought I might tip over and cook to death on the pavement, like an egg frying in a pan. The screen door banged open and the old lady stood there with a tray in her hands.

"Come have a cookie and some lemonade," she said.

I thought I heard angelic music somewhere. I stumbled onto the porch and fell into a chair.

"My name is Mae," she said.

I drained the lemonade in one go. Mae filled it for me again.

"I'm James," I said. "Please, don't call me Jim."

She smiled. "All right, James. Thank you for helping me today. I can't get around like I used to."

I nodded as I stuffed a chocolate chip cookie into my mouth. The warm sweetness melted on my tongue, and I closed my eyes to revel in the divine pleasure.

"I'm afraid I let it go for a few months," she said.

Her gaze strayed to the lawn. A strange, bleak expression passed over her face before she looked back at me.

"You're not from around here, are you?" she said.

I shook my head. "Idaho," I mumbled over another cookie.

She nodded. "I thought I heard an accent."

I wasn't going to tell her that *she* was the one with an accent. Everybody down here had one.

"Not many white boys would volunteer to help an old black woman without being asked."

I shrugged. I didn't want to tell her I was such a loser I had ridden by the first time and that I had been regretting my decision to help her.

"What grade are you in?" she asked.

"Seventh."

She nodded. "I teach at the grade school—fifth grade."

I stared at her. A teacher? Was it even legal for her to talk to a kid during summer vacation? I glanced back at the chewed up remains of the weeds and wondered why a teacher with an injured leg was trying to mow a lawn.

"Where's your husband?" I asked.

But as soon as the words left my mouth, I regretted them. Her brow fell into a frown.

"He's traveling," she mumbled. Then, she fell silent and stared at her glass.

I realized I had overstayed my welcome, so I excused myself and headed for home.

CHAPTER EIGHT
THE KILL ZONE

That man was probably dumped there by some mafia thug," Mom fumed. "I don't want you down there."

The story about the anonymous caller cycled through on the evening news for a solid week. Every time it came on, Mom freaked out.

"It's a park," I protested.

"It's a crime scene," she said. "You stay close to the house."

"I have to pass the park to deliver my papers."

Mom opened her mouth, turned pink in the face, and stammered something about preferring small Idaho towns. Since she worked the graveyard shift and slept most of the day, she couldn't always keep track of me. Still, Mom was right. The police would be waiting for me. I knew it. And because I knew I shouldn't go anywhere near that creek, I had to go near the creek.

The area was still roped off with yellow tape, so I sat on the swing, trying to act like I had no idea a dead body had lain moldering in the creek bed. Damon's wallet bulged in my pocket, and my gaze strayed to the bridge and the yellow tape that marked the forbidden territory. I kept the wallet on me all the time so Mom wouldn't find it and just in case I found the opportunity to get rid of it. What if I ran down there real fast and stuffed the wallet back under the rock? Would anybody know?

I stood up to make a dash for the creek when that lop-eared dog came bounding from the brush along the bank. He clutched a dirty baseball in his mouth that had turned a weird shade of blackish brown. I figured he had been down there snooping around where Damon had lain. He headed straight for me, so I picked up a rock.

"Get outta here," I yelled.

That dumb dog had been nothing but trouble. I cocked back my arm to chuck it at him when a police car rolled around the corner, its tires crunching gravel. I dropped back into the swing, trying to act like I was some innocent little kid. Maybe the cop would drive on by. But no. The car stopped.

I couldn't breathe. I jerked my head around looking for an escape route, but he had already seen me. I was a goner.

The officer slammed his car door and stomped right up to me. The big black baton swung at his belt. I peered up into his solemn face and wilted. He glared at me for a minute. Then he glanced at the slobbering dog, whose tail beat the earth like he was a drummer.

"Everything all right?" he asked.

Well, that wasn't what I expected. I kept waiting for him to whip out his baton and thump me on the head.

I blinked and nodded. "Yes, sir."

"See anything unusual around here in the last few weeks?"

I swallowed. "Uh."

"Like any strangers hanging around, strange cars, kids throwing baseballs at parked cars." He glanced at the dog again and the filthy baseball the dog dropped at my feet. "Anything like that?"

I licked my lips. "I don't think so."

He nodded, but I could tell he didn't believe me. I was a horrible liar.

"Okay," he said. "You should be careful around here alone. It might not be safe anymore."

"Yes, sir," I said.

He strode off to his car and drove away. I fell off the back of the swing onto the red earth and laid there staring up at the cloudless sky. I was so deep in the doo-doo now I could smell it. And my twelve-year-old brain wasn't helping me figure out how to get out of it.

The dog licked my face. I swatted him away. Every time something went wrong that dumb dog was there.

When I rode past Mae's house the next day, she raised a hand in my direction. I thought it was a wave, so I waved back. But I didn't stop. I hadn't forgotten that she worked as a teacher, and I had offended her by asking about her husband. I wasn't sure what she might do. She could smash me into a Pop-Tart if she wanted, so it was best to keep my distance. Students weren't supposed to see teachers during the summer break anyway. It wasn't natural. It went against every code ever invented to protect childhood.

I peddled home and lounged around the TV, trying to avoid my conscience. But it wouldn't leave me alone. I grabbed my BB gun and waited for a mouse to stick its head out from behind the couch. After Mom's encounter with the mouse, she swore Clint and me to the solemn duty of killing every mouse we could find, so we invented a sick game to let us kill mice and still watch TV.

Our house didn't have a basement, but it had a crawl space that seemed to breed mice, and they got into everything. We baited a trap with cheese and set it right behind the couch where we could see it if we sat off to the side of the room. We watched *Twilight Zone* or *Gilligan's Island* while keeping one eye on the trap. When a mouse approached the cheese with his black nose twitching, we blasted away, just like a war zone. BBs flew everywhere. Blood splattered the walls. Mice bodies piled up.

Once we'd blown their brains out, we saved them for when Mom woke up. A mouse held real close to her face always got a violent and hilarious reaction. Her eyes grew wide. Her mouth opened. Her hands balled into fists. Her feet started pumping. The shriek began to build.

That's when we ran for it because, after the first shriek, Mom's fists started flying. She wasn't trying to hurt us. It was just her primeval survival instinct kicking into high gear.

Today the hunting was no good, so I carried my BB gun outside with a bunch of green plastic army men. I set up the army men in the dirt and shot at them like I was some GI in Vietnam. Right in the middle of my little war, a red cardinal swooped into the tree right above my army men. Without even thinking, I swept my gun up, aimed, and squeezed the trigger. The cardinal jumped into the air in a flutter of wings and crashed to the ground where it flapped in a circle for a few seconds before it lay twitching and quivering in the dust.

I bounded to my feet and raced to it with a whoop of triumph, like the point man that had just saved his platoon from a sniper. But when I came up to the bird, my heart dropped into my shoes, and all the whoop went out of me.

It was beautiful. Bright red feathers, tinted black, glimmered in the afternoon sun. A black mask surrounded its red beak, which opened and closed a few times as if it were asking me why I killed it. The red crest on top of its head swept the dirt as it twitched and quivered.

I knelt beside it, remembering the first time I saw Damon lying against that log. Was Mom right? Had he been shot down like the cardinal by some murderous thug who dumped him in the creek? Was I just as bad as a murdering thug because I still had the wallet?

A crushing wave of remorse pressed down upon me, making it hard to breathe. What had I done? I had killed an innocent bird for no reason—because I was bored. I trudged to the garage and got the shovel before carrying the cardinal to the back of the yard by the fence and dug a little hole. I placed the bird in the hole and folded its wings around its body. The cardinal looked so small and vulnerable. After I packed the soil back down and stuck a stick in the ground to mark the grave, I knelt in the dirt staring at it.

Death had never been so real to me before that moment. I had murdered plenty of mice, but I figured they deserved it since they ate holes in our clothes and built nests in our food. Until then, Damon had been just a cool corpse. Now, I realized like I hadn't before that he had been a real person. Somebody would want to know what happened to him. Somebody would miss him. I was the only person in the entire world who knew his name. That's when I knew what I needed do.

I had to return the wallet somehow. Just taking it back to the creek wasn't enough. If it belonged to the guy in the creek, the police needed to know. So I set about trying to figure out how to get the wallet to the police without them knowing I was the one that had found it and that I had called them about the body. There was no way they would believe I hadn't stolen it off his dead body, or worse, that I hadn't killed him just to get the money.

Every time I thought about going to the police station to hand them the wallet, my hands grew sweaty, and a swooping heat rushed through my stomach. When I tried to walk into the kitchen and hand it to Mom, I got weak in the knees. She would be disappointed in me. I couldn't stand it when she gave me that sad frown that said I had failed.

The spell of all those green bills still gripped me. My family needed money. That dead guy didn't, so I let the summer slip away as I planned and schemed and delayed. One week turned into two, and I couldn't figure out how to do it. I lived with the constant fear the police would trace the wallet back to me if I gave it to them, and they would throw me in the slammer for the rest of my life.

When the last week of summer crept up, I knew I had to bite the bullet. I packed up the wallet in a nice envelope with the letter I pecked out with two fingers on my dad's typewriter. The letter explained that I found the wallet in the creek all by itself before I found the body and that I thought it might belong to the dead guy they had been asking about.

It wasn't completely honest, but I was trying to make sure I did the right thing without being punished for something I didn't do. I addressed the letter to the police department and rode my bike to the post office clear up on the college campus.

This time, I didn't fool around. I wiped everything down with a towel before sending it. I wasn't stupid. Well, when I tried to stuff the envelope with the bulging wallet, my own hands betrayed me. They jerked and spasmed so badly I couldn't get the money in the envelope.

In the end, I gave up and sent the wallet all by itself with the letter. It was better than nothing. Besides, I didn't *know* the money belonged to the dead guy. I was just guessing. And if he had been a thug, like Mom said, then he'd probably stolen it anyway. If the police could find Damon's family, at least they could tell them what happened to him. That was what mattered.

CHAPTER NINE
A GOOD BEATING FOR
THE NEW KIDS

As the new kid in town, the first day of school could not be a pleasant experience. To start with, no one got my name right. In my case, it couldn't be hard. It's pronounced the way it's spelled. And yet, by the time the letters J A M E S passed from the page through the eye, reached the brain, and came out the mouth, they mysteriously transformed into J I M. It didn't make any sense. No one would take some kid named Carson and call him Cis. So I couldn't see why people did that to the name James.

I was sensitive about this because I had been traumatized by my first baseball coach at the tender age of six. One practice, I was standing out in left field waiting for it to start when the coach screamed at someone named Jim to move over. I just stood there waiting. After a few tries, he stomped out, glared down at my trembling little body, and growled at me.

"I told you to move over, Jim."

I peered up at him and squeaked, "But my name is James."

Every teacher asked us to correct them if they mispronounced our names and then they called me Jim. When I raised my hand and asked them to call me James, they just frowned like I had done something wrong.

I avoided trouble until science class in the third period, when I found a pile of torn papers on my desk in the front row. Any child with a normal brain would have swept them off into his hand and thrown them away. But not me. I flipped them off, one at a time. Of course, one of them caught air, soared as graceful as a bird right up to the teacher's desk, turned a little somersault, and landed right on the paper he was reading. His head snapped up. Our gazes locked. I knew I was in trouble.

Mr. Ward pointed at me and bent his big finger to tell me to come to his desk. I walked up to him, and he pointed to the door. I shuffled into the hallway wondering what to expect until he came out with the biggest, nastiest paddle I'd ever seen. It looked like a flat baseball bat with holes drilled in it. It was definitely a two-hander.

"Empty your back pockets, turn around, and grab your ankles," he said.

He glared at me when I opened my mouth to explain that I hadn't meant to flip the paper at him. He snapped the board against his palm. I grabbed my ankles, which is probably the most humiliating thing you can make a person do. It's true, I had been stupid, but if they spanked us for little things like this, what would they do if we really broke the rules? Cut off our hands and brand us with a hot iron?

The paddle whistled a high, ominous shriek like a banshee rushing in for the kill and smacked my backside. I fell flat on my face and slid a good five feet down the hallway. My backside felt like I'd been slammed with a red-hot poker. As I crawled to my feet, I blinked as fast as I could to keep the tears in.

"One more—just to make sure you don't forget," he snapped.

What could I do? Make a break for it?

The paddle whistled and smacked, but this time I braced for it. I only stumbled a few steps, but my whole backside was on fire. I glanced back, expecting to see flames and smell smoke.

"There's more where that came from," he said, wagging the paddle at me. "So, don't get any ideas that you'll get special treatment from me just because you're new."

Oh, I had ideas all right, but most of them were of revenge and murder. The other ideas were confused. I'd been spanked at school once before in Idaho after I sneaked off to the candy store with a bunch of friends. That time they used a strap from a car tire. But I deserved that one. I had knowingly broken a school rule.

When I came in to sit down on my tender backside, everybody, black, white, and anywhere in between, watched me. One Hispanic kid in the back looked sympathetic, but everybody else perched on the edge of their seats like vultures leering over a fresh kill. I guess they wanted to see me cry, but I would not start a new school year as a crybaby.

I was standing in the lunch line when the crash of a plastic tray rang over the chatter of the students. A hush fell over the lunchroom as everyone spun to see what happened.

"Cracker," someone screamed. Then the kids were rushing to get out of the way as a black girl and a white boy rolled around at our feet. At first, I thought she was mad because he stole her cracker. Then, remembering the way the kids treated me at the baseball tryouts, I wondered if cracker was supposed to be an insult. A teacher waded in and pried them apart. The boy spat blood, and the girl sported a split lip.

"Never talk to me again, you honky cracker," the girl snarled.

That sounded funny, and I smiled. What the heck was a honky cracker? It sounded like some disgusting new candy bar or the name of a cowboy's horse. I stopped smiling when I caught a teacher glaring at me. I ducked my head and slipped into the crowd. Sometimes anonymity was best.

After the fight, I tried to play basketball with some white kids, but this tall kid kept bouncing the ball off the top of my head pretending he was dribbling, so I gave up.

I spent the rest of the lunch break watching all of those histories play themselves out. A group of boys and girls paired off and wandered around the playground holding hands. A few couples wedged themselves in the gaps between the walls of the buildings to make out. Some Hispanic boys played marbles and argued about the rules of shooting. I tried to figure out who Darth Vader was, but it was a toss-up between this wiry black kid named Leroy who sported a huge afro and a white kid named Oscar who had a flat face with a butch haircut and bulging muscles.

Leroy led a pack of black boys and girls who tossed a tennis ball against the wall in some kind of game. Oscar played basketball for a while before he roamed around looking for little kids to pick on. I noticed that he only picked on white kids or Hispanics—but never the black kids. If he came close to one. Leroy and his gang would make their way towards him until Oscar veered off to pick on some white kid again.

This all made me nervous. I didn't understand it. I searched the area for the Obi-Wan Kenobi who could explain what was going on, but I never found one.

In band class, they gave me a trumpet that looked like it had been through the Civil War. It sounded like a giraffe sneezing when I tried to play it.

When I made it home, Mom was already awake and waiting for us with a plate of warm cookies. My heart swelled with gratitude for her. After the day I had had, a few cookies were just what I needed.

"How was your first day?" she asked with a nervous, hopeful smile. I knew she worried about us. She wanted us to make friends and to be happy like we had been in Idaho.

I shrugged.

"Did you meet any nice people?"

I shrugged again. Her smile faded. She laid a hand on my arm. "You'll make friends, Honey. Give it time."

I had made friends all right, with a big, long paddle. My sister, Dawn, came in grinning from ear to ear and swooning about some heartthrob who held the door for her. Things got interesting when Clint slouched into the front room. Mom took one look at him and lunged to her feet, scattering the plate of cookies all over the floor.

"My word," she breathed. "What happened to you?"

Clint scowled and looked away. His face had changed color like some alien from *Star Wars*. Bruises in several shades of black and blue covered his face. One eye sported a huge shiner and had swollen shut. The pocket had been torn off his blue Levi jacket. Mom scrambled for a bag of ice while I rescued the cookies before the mice could find them. She made Clint sit on the couch and hold the ice to his eye.

"Who did this?" she demanded. My mother didn't get mad easily, but the idea of someone hurting one of her kids was enough to give her that wild-eyed, mother-tiger look.

Clint shrugged.

"Tell me who did it," she demanded. "I'll call the school."

"You wanna get me killed?" Clint asked.

Mom just stared at him, slack-jawed and confused. The fire went out of her.

"It's the first day of school, Mom. This happens every time."

Mom gazed at me and Dawn as tears welled up in her eyes. Lines of worry spread over her face.

"Don't lie," Clint said. "You both got picked on today too, didn't you?"

We exchanged shamefaced glances.

"See?" he said. "When you're new, you're a target." He threw the ice pack on the couch. "I have to get my papers delivered."

Mom was weepy the rest of the evening, so I didn't tell her about the paddling. It would only make it worse. I wanted to comfort her, but I didn't know what to say. The truth might hurt her more than the silence.

CHAPTER TEN
SNAKE IN THE GRASS

Mae was just getting home when I approached her house that evening. I almost rode by, but on an impulse, I pulled into her driveway behind her.

She glanced up at me a little surprised, I think.

I gestured toward the weed patch that was starting to get thick again.

"I can mow that for you, if you want," I said, surprising myself with the offer. The pain of the last mowing was still fresh in my mind. Maybe I did it because Mae was the only friend I had.

She smiled. "That would be nice, James." She talked like a teacher, but at least she called me by my real name.

"I'll come back after I finish my route," I said.

She nodded and hefted a big bag of books. She limped a little as she headed for the house.

When I finished delivering my papers, I dragged the lawn mower out of her garage and jerked the cord. The mower coughed. It didn't want to start, but I kept at it until it roared to life. I leaned into it and began the battle once again. Most of the grass had fallen to the mower when something jerked on the tail of my T-shirt. I glanced around to find that stupid lop-eared dog. He had come out of nowhere, grabbed my shirt in his mouth, and tugged on it.

"Good grief," I said. "Would you leave me alone?"

I kicked at him, but he just bounded away and then hopped back in to nip at my pant legs. He thought it was great fun, but I wanted to ram that mower right down his throat. We went at it like this for a while until he stopped pouncing in and out and started barking at the last patch of weeds I still had to mow.

"Get out of the way," I yelled as I almost ran over his paw. He ignored me. I pushed ahead, trying to shoo him out of the way, when something big and black stirred in the weeds. At first, I thought the heat had warped my brain and that it was just a branch or something shimmering in a heat haze. When the thing raised its head and jumped at the lawn mower, I couldn't keep the scream in.

The writhing monster sank its teeth into the tire and curled its body around it. The more it curled, the bigger it got. I was too freaked out to let go of the mower. Instead, I jerked it around, trying to dislodge the beast while the lawn mower roared and the dog barked and I screamed. I don't know what I was thinking—maybe I wasn't.

Mae loomed out of nowhere, slapped me on the back of the head to get me to shut up, and stabbed at the writhing mass with a shovel. The blade sliced through its tail. The snake let go of the wheel and reared toward Mae. Its mouth opened wide—the inside white as cotton. Long fangs dripped some clear liquid. Its head swayed. The dog went crazy snapping at the snake but too scared to get in close.

I thought Mae was a goner for sure. Unless she had some serious Jedi skills, I couldn't see how she could survive this battle with nothing but a shovel. I raised the lawn mower up, its blade whirling, and barreled toward the snake.

The mower jerked like I had hit a big rock. Bits and pieces of snake sprayed everywhere like a geyser going off. The mower coughed to a stop. An ear-shattering silence rushed in upon the scene. The air smelled of cut grass, gasoline, and guts. Mae didn't stir. She had frozen in place with the shovel clutched in both hands as if it were a baseball bat. I retched as the bile rose in my throat.

"Merciful heaven," Mae breathed.

Snake guts dripped off her legs. She turned to gape at me.

"You tangled with a cottonmouth, boy," she said. "What's got into your head?"

"I didn't do anything," I said. "It just came out of nowhere and attacked the lawn mower."

"Your dog tried to warn you," she said.

"He's not my dog," I protested. "Every time he comes around something bad happens to me."

Mae surveyed me from head to foot and glanced down at her own legs where bits of snake speckled her brown skin. She took a deep breath. "Well, we can't go inside like this," she said.

She dragged out the garden hose and sprayed me down. The water from the hose was warm, but it still felt deliciously cool after I'd been baking in my sweat while I mowed the lawn. I think Mae enjoyed herself because that stream of water somehow kept hitting me in the face—even though my face wasn't dirty.

She gave herself and the dog the same treatment. The dog tried to catch the fountain of water in its mouth and ran circles around Mae. She laughed, but she didn't give up until she had sprayed him down. He shook the water from his thick coat and padded up to nose at Mae's hand. She stroked his wet fur.

"He sure seems to like you," she said. "If he's not yours, whose is he?"

"I don't know. He just showed up at the ballpark and made me look like an idiot during the tryouts. It's his fault they put me on the D team."

Mae gave me a knowing smile that said she didn't believe me before she climbed up the steps to sit on the porch. Water dripped from her curly black hair. She had already brought out the lemonade and cookies, so I helped myself as the water pooled around our feet.

That soaking sure felt good, and so did the ice-cold lemonade that ran down my throat and cooled my insides. I let the dog gulp down bits of my cookies, but I wouldn't pat him. I didn't care if he saw the snake first. He had ruined my tryouts and somehow led the police to the creek when I was trying to put the wallet back.

Mae sat quietly as if she remembered something sad, and I considered how brave she had been around the snake. Most girls I knew would have shrieked and booked it at the mere sight of a black slithering monster like that.

"How come you weren't scared of the snake?" I asked.

She appraised me shrewdly. "Who said I wasn't afraid?"

42

"Well, you just went after it with that shovel like a Jedi, so I thought—"

"Look," Mae said. "I'm a southern girl, James. No southern girl can afford to be squeamish about bugs and snakes. You'd die a thousand deaths if you were. But that doesn't mean I go looking for them either." She gave me a meaningful lifting of her eyebrows. "But when you've got to deal with one, it's best to just deal with it."

"My mom's scared of mice," I said.

Mae sniffed. "Don't know any woman who wants them in her house."

"Can I ask you a question?" I said.

Mae nodded and sipped her lemonade. The dog curled up at my feet after he decided I wasn't going to give him any more cookies.

"How come the black kids and the white kids don't play with each other at school?"

Mae seemed like the right person to ask. She was a teacher, and she was black.

She stopped smiling. I thought I had offended her again. But she set her glass on the table and studied me real hard.

"You ever heard of segregation?" she asked.

I heard Dad talk about it once because he grew up in Texas. But I couldn't remember much about it. I shook my head.

"Hmm. Okay. Let me make this easy for you."

I nodded. That was always a good idea for a kid with a twelve-year-old brain.

"You've heard of slavery?"

"Yeah."

"Well, in this country, some white folks who lost their slaves after the Civil War didn't want to let the black folks become normal citizens. They were afraid, so they created a bunch of laws to make sure the black people couldn't compete for jobs—that they couldn't get an education. They tried to keep the black folks from eating at the same restaurants and drinking from the same drinking fountains."

That's what Dad told me, but I didn't remember him explaining it.

"But why?" I asked.

Mae shook her head. "Some folks just need to feel superior to someone else. It's all about power and greed."

"But no kid at school is gonna get power by *not* playing with the other kids," I said.

Mae gave me a sad smile. "In their own heads they do."

I wrinkled my brow in confusion. "I don't get it," I said. "It didn't look like the black kids wanted to play with the white kids any more than the white kids wanted to play with the black kids. I even saw a black girl beat the tar out of some white kid today."

"Well, they probably didn't want to play together," Mae sighed. "It's going to be hard for you to understand because you haven't experienced discrimination before. For a long time, blacks were picked on and abused. They used to hang black men and women in public and burn down black schools. It was dangerous to be black. In fact, in some places it still is."

I frowned and stuffed a cookie into my mouth. How had I missed all of this?

"My husband and I," Mae continued, "were civil rights workers back in the fifties and sixties. We fought long and hard to get the discriminatory laws revoked." Her brow wrinkled. I thought she looked sad. "When you come back, I'll pull out some of my pictures if you want to look at them."

I nodded and stood up.

"Sorry about the mess," I said.

I glanced at the ruins of the snake still spread across the lawn.

"It'll give the ants something to eat," she said. A deep, resonating laugh boiled out of her that seemed to come right from the center of her soul. "I haven't had such a good time in a long while."

Sleep wouldn't come for me that night—but not because of the stifling heat and the sticky sheets that clung to my body. I was struggling to understand what Mae meant by discrimination. If she just meant getting picked on, then I understood that pretty well. But most of what I experienced didn't seem to have anything to do with the color of my skin. White kids and black kids picked on me with equal pleasure. Maybe they were just trying to be fair or something.

I could hear that Clint hadn't fallen asleep because he wasn't breathing like a bull moose, so I decided to ask him how he managed to get into a fight at school. Maybe he knew something about discrimination I didn't.

"Hey, Clint," I said. "You awake?"

"I am now," he grunted.

"What happened?" I asked. "I mean, how did you get into a fight?"

He sighed. "Some punk shoved me into a locker, so I had to hit him."

"You *had* to?"

"Yep. If you let anybody get away with something like that, it's only gonna get worse."

"Why?"

"Don't be stupid," he said. "You've been a new kid before. Every bully in the school sees you as fresh meat. They've already picked on all the other kids. The ones that are too weak to fight back are the ones they keep going after. You fight back, and they'll leave you alone."

"Doesn't look like you won the fight," I said.

"I didn't," Clint said. "He was a boxer."

"Wow. That was some kind of stupid to a pick a fight with a boxer."

"Nah. He thumped on me, but I got in a few good ones. He won't bother me anymore and neither will most of the other jerks."

"But you lost," I said. "Doesn't that make you more of a target?"

Clint grunted. "Sometimes I wonder if you missed the announcement when God was handing out brains. What did I just tell you? If you let them hit you once, they're gonna do it again and again. You never let 'em hit you and get away with it. You understand?"

"I guess so."

This didn't make a lot of sense to me, but he was older. He ought to know.

CHAPTER ELEVEN
MURDER IN THE CLASSROOM

Quiet!" someone bellowed.

I scanned the classroom, trying to figure out who would dare scream so loud in our first art class, but all I could see was a blonde head bobbing up and down between the rows of students. I didn't realize it was the teacher until she climbed onto a high stool and peered down at us through thick, horn-rimmed glasses. She looked like a little bird sitting on a perch. I smiled until she bellowed again.

"Quiet!" Her voice boomed like a foghorn.

Silence descended as we all stared in shock. How could someone so small make so much noise?

"My name is Mrs. Took," she roared. "In this class, we're going to explore your creativity—your inner artist."

A murmur swept through the class. Heads turned.

"Some of you," she continued, "may have been told that successful art is the product of pure talent. But I'm here to tell you that this is a lie. Artistic sensitivity can be learned. If you don't believe me, take a look at these two paintings."

She clicked a button on her slide projector. An image appeared on the big, white screen hanging from the ceiling. People sat in silence for a moment before they began to snigger. The picture confused me. It looked like someone had crossbred an elephant with a giraffe, or maybe a pumpkin with a carrot. I tilted my head sideways to see if a different perspective might help. But it didn't do any good. That was one ugly picture.

"What is the subject of this painting?" Mrs. Took asked.

Confused students glanced around at one another. Someone raised her hand.

"It's an alien?"

Mrs. Took shook her head.

"It's an elephant on a swing."

"No," Mrs. Took said. "It's a bowl of fruit."

"No, it isn't," someone else blurted.

Mrs. Took smiled down on the kid as he turned red.

"Now, take a look at this painting."

A second painting appeared beside the first. It was a landscape with an elegant canoe skimming across the surface of a mirrored lake. This painting was so beautiful that it made my heart ache.

"What's the subject of this painting?" Mrs. Took asked.

A few people answered, but she always shook her head.

"No," she said. "It's the effect of light on water."

"How were we supposed to know that?" someone said.

Mrs. Took ignored her.

"Now, can you guess who painted these paintings?"

After a round of answers that ranged from Picasso to Rembrandt, Mrs. Took smiled down upon us from her perch.

"I did," she said. "Though I'm flattered you would think otherwise. I painted the first one in a seventh-grade art class. The last one I sold two years ago for fifteen thousand dollars."

Exclamations of disbelief smothered anything else she might have said.

After she bellowed again, we all turned to listen to her.

"As you can see," she said, "I have no native talent, but I learned how to paint, and so can you."

These words sent a spark of interest surging through my weak, little brain. I had been trying to draw for years, but, every time I drew a horse, it looked more like a deformed pig. I had long despaired of ever moving beyond coloring inside the lines and scratching out stick figures.

This despair did not spring from a mere lack of confidence. I spent the last six years dreading class art projects. Not only were my projects unrecognizable, but all my teachers hung my picture beside the girl whose artwork came out perfect every time. Day after day, I had to walk in and see a piece of junk with my name on it pinned to the wall next to the divine art of some future female Michael Angelo. Man, that was depressing.

But Mrs. Took inspired me. When she started us on circles and ovals and then turned them into animals, I couldn't believe it. For the first time in my life, the pig I drew actually looked like a pig, not some mutant reject of a nuclear explosion.

"Most of you will die before the year is out," Mr. Sentury, our World History teacher, said as he twirled a ruler in his hand. He wore a Hawaiian shirt with khaki shorts, big sandals, and socks pulled up to his knees. He looked like an oversized kindergartner in that get-up. The worst thing, though, was the way he wiped his nose. He started at the palm of his hand and dragged his nose all the way up his arm to the elbow. The wet stain on his arm made me gag.

We all exchanged glances.

"I will usually give you the opportunity to select your method of death," he said. "But sometimes I will be forced to choose for you."

Then, he launched into a discussion about human evolution that ended with the extinction of the Neanderthals. When he finished, he pointed to me.

"You," he said. "You're going to die first. Come up here."

My eyes popped open, my heart skipped a few beats and started thumping like a drum. I gulped and rose to my feet.

"Hurry up," he said. "I don't have all day."

I shuffled to the front of the room, painfully aware of the dead silence that descended over the classroom. Only the ticking of the clock and the whoosh of the air ventilation system could be heard. Mr. Sentury shoved a broom into my hands.

"You're a Neanderthal hunting a woolly mammoth. You throw your spear," he gestured for me to throw it, so I did. The broom sailed through the air, knocked the globe off the table, and clattered to the floor.

"The mammoth bellows in rage and charges," he said. "What do you do?"

I glanced around and shrugged.

His hands dropped to his sides. He gave me that look teachers give when they want to say how stupid they think you are but know they can't.

"You'd shrug at it? Really?"

"I don't know," I said.

"You grab your spear and turn to face it because you're no coward. You're a caveman." He stared at me as if he expected me to do something. Then, his lips puckered.

"I need you to help me out here," he said.

"Oh," I said. I grabbed the broom. A few kids snickered.

"The mammoth bellows in rage, and you thrust your spear forward."

I poked the spear toward him.

"But it's no good. Your spear breaks, and the mammoth gores you through the chest and tosses you over its head. You land in a crumpled heap."

He waited until I was curled up on the cold floor.

"The mammoth stomps on you until you're as flat as a pancake." He raised his sandaled foot and pantomimed stepping on me. "Your friends and family find you all smashed on the frozen ground. Because they have human-sized brains and a belief in the afterlife, they take you and place your body in a cave."

He waved for the class to join us. By now, they figured out we were playacting, so they all came to the front of the room. He gestured for the boys to pick me up and set me on his desk.

"The women are weeping," he waved a hand at them like a choir director. None of them made a sound. They stared around at each other as if they were convinced Mr. Sentury was crazy. He clicked his tongue at the girls' refusal to weep properly before gesturing to the boys.

"The men place your hunting spear and stone knife beside you to go with you into the afterlife."

He handed the broom and a piece of chalk to the boys who placed them in my hands.

"They all bowed down and sang the death song."

Everybody stared at him. No one wanted to sing.

"Oh, all right," he said. "You can just moan and groan."

That was more like it. One wiry kid burst out in a loud groan and soon the entire class joined in until the room sounded like a herd of sick cows. Mr. Sentury seemed to enjoy the noise for a bit, then he waved them back to their seats. When I tried to sit up, he pushed me back down.

"Your body rots and decays until all that's left is your crushed skull. Some scientist digs you up, and from the shape of your skull, determines that Neanderthals could speak."

"I heard Neanderthals had bigger brains than humans," some white girl said. "And since Europeans descended from them, that's what made Europeans smarter."

Mr. Sentury twirled his ruler and frowned.

"Come up here," he said. He pointed to one of the black kids. "You," he said.

As the two of them stepped nervously to the front of the room, Mr. Sentury yanked a tape measure from the drawer of his desk. He pulled it around the white girl's head. "Exactly twenty-one inches around. Now you." Mr. Sentury measured the black kid's head. "Yep, just over twenty-two inches around."

He raised his eyebrows at the white girl. "Based on these measurements, who has the largest brain here?"

The girl frowned but didn't answer.

"Exactly," Mr. Sentury said. "Take your seats."

He waited until they slumped down in their chairs before continuing.

"Brain size isn't necessarily a sign of intelligence. We have evidence that modern Europeans may share DNA with Neanderthals." He ran his arm up his nose. "Some people can't accept the fact that we are all Africans. There is no evidence that our species evolved anywhere but in Africa. When Homo sapiens arrived in Europe, they had better technology than the Neanderthals and eventually replaced them. It had nothing to do with brain size because modern humans have smaller brains than the Neanderthals did."

The girl didn't look convinced, and some white boys kept glancing at the black kids with little sneers. I thought they might decide to fight it out right there in class on the first day.

Mr. Sentury picked up his ruler and twirled it again. He shooed me off the desk where I still lay in my death pose. I shuffled to my seat.

"The story we have been telling today," Mr. Sentury said, "is about our relationship as members of the same species. Scientists now challenge the idea of separate races, which may not even exist scientifically. We are all Africans and only those that want to persist in racist explanations for some supposed European racial superiority deny it."

When several boys protested, Mr. Sentury raised his ruler and waved it to cut them off.

"We have also been telling a story about courage," he continued. "Courage to venture into the unknown. We are not the only species to possess courage. But today, we are the only species to crave power for power's sake. We are the only species that seeks domination for the sheer pleasure of exercising control over other people. As we shall see, humans have been driven to seek power from the beginning, and some have had the courage to resist it."

I wondered if what Mr. Sentury said explained what I saw on the playground and what Mae had been saying about discrimination. If it did, I still didn't understand why kids would do it.

CHAPTER TWELVE
TENNIS BALLS AND
PHOTO ALBUMS

I died the first day of history class, but that's not what nearly got me killed. I was standing in line at lunch when Oscar, the flat-faced white kid with the butch haircut, crowded right in front of me.

"Hey," I said. "Cutting is against the rules." The protest popped out of my mouth before I could stop it.

Oscar turned. "Who made you the lunchroom police?"

I shrugged. "You can't crowd."

I was stubborn about these things, though I knew I was in deep trouble again.

"Who's going to stop me?"

I didn't say anything.

"That's what I thought." He turned his back.

Just then, two more boys came over to join him.

"Hey," I said.

One jerk cutting in line was bad enough, but three meant I would miss more of recess. They all turned as one.

"Who's the big mouth?" one of them asked. He scowled at me. "You gonna go tattle, like a baby?"

Oscar poked his finger in my chest. "Watch yourself, smarty pants." His gaze scanned my entire body. "You must be one of

52

those free-lunch kids."

I still didn't say anything because I knew Mom talked to someone about a reduced lunch for us. My mind kept going over what Clint said. If he hit me, I had to hit him back, and then I would get killed. He laughed, and I stood there, knowing I had been stupid and angry I wasn't big enough to shove a lunch tray all the way up his pug nose.

At recess, I sat around watching people again until I got bored and decided to join a weird game I heard the boys call "Butts-Up." I watched long enough to figure out the rules—more or less. You threw a tennis ball against the wall. When it bounced back, someone had to catch it with one hand. If the ball touched them and they didn't catch it, they had to run to the wall and touch it before someone threw the ball and hit them. If they got hit five times, they had to stand with their hands on the wall and their back to the crowd. Each boy then had a free shot at the kid's backside. Hence, the name Butts-Up.

Since I could catch a baseball, I figured I might do all right at this game. I tried the white boys first, but Oscar told me to take a hike. I went to the black kids next. Leroy, the boy with the big afro, caught the ball and turned to gaze at me. He studied me for a moment and then smirked.

"You wanna play with us?" he questioned.

I nodded.

He glanced over my head toward Oscar and the white kids. A little smile played on his lips.

"Suit yourself," he said.

Then, he barked an unfriendly laugh, and I wondered if this was a good idea. I did okay at the game, but I didn't realize that if the ball bounced off your shoe, even if you weren't trying to catch it, you had to run.

Leroy picked up the ball and chucked it at me as hard as he could even though I was only a few feet away from him. It hit me clean in the face. I stumbled backward as the pain flared on my cheek and tears sprung to my eyes. Man, that stung like the devil.

"You have to run if the ball touches you," he said.

It took me a few seconds to get my eyesight back. The ball hit me two more times before I stumbled up to lay a hand on the wall. As the game went on, some boys rushed in front of me and acted like they would catch the ball only to let it go so I didn't have time to get out of the way. Soon I had five points against me, and I slumped up to the red brick wall and placed my hands on it. The brick was rough and scratched my palms as I jerked with each strike of the ball.

Either those kids couldn't throw worth beans, or they weren't trying very hard to hit my backside. The ball hit me in the head more than it did my bottom. I swear some of them got back in line after they threw because that line wasn't getting any shorter. I decided to leave when someone shouted.

"Hey!"

I craned my head around.

Leroy picked up the ball. He faced Oscar, the flat-faced white kid. The sneer on his lips told me I was looking at a lot of history I didn't know, and I would pay for my ignorance. These two had clearly arrived at some kind of truce, but they were still wary of each other.

"What are you doing?" Oscar demanded.

Leroy shrugged and stabbed a thumb in my direction. "He wanted to play," he said, "but he's a lousy catch."

Well, that wasn't true, but this didn't seem like the right time to correct him. I dropped my hands from the wall and stood with my back to it, watching to see how this galactic battle would play out.

Oscar's lips lifted in a snarl as he glared at me. "What's the matter with you?" he demanded. "Get outta here. Don't embarrass us again."

What did he mean "us"? I wasn't sure what to do, so I stood there. Oscar chucked a tennis ball at me. I ducked.

"I said get outta here!" he yelled.

Now seemed like a good time to make an exit, so I trudged away, trying not to limp because of the new charley horse in my leg. I didn't have a clue what the entire episode even meant, and no one was going to tell me.

When I got home from school, I found my little sister playing in the front yard in nothing but her diaper. I couldn't blame her. It was hot. I would have stripped down to my birthday suit if I wouldn't have fried to death in the sun. I scooped her up and deposited her on the couch where Mom was doing laundry and keeping an eye on my sister through the screen door.

I folded my papers, while my little sister helped Mom fold the clothes by scattering them all over the floor. Then I rode off to my paper route, pumping the peddles as the paper bag swung from my handlebars. Mae sat on her porch as if she had been waiting for me. I waved at her as I passed, but I needed to get my papers delivered first. When I peddled past again on my way home, she motioned for me to come over.

I thumped up the stairs.

"How was school?" she asked.

I shrugged as I slid into a chair. "Okay, I guess."

"Doesn't sound okay."

"I have another question for you," I said.

"Shoot." She leaned back and settled into her chair.

"I tried to play with the black kids today, but they were just as mean as the white kids. Then, a white kid told me to stop embarrassing the white kids. I don't get it."

Mae gave me a sad, pitying frown.

"Boy, you have landed yourself in the middle of a lot of history. It doesn't have anything to do with you. The white boy said you were embarrassing them because you were playing with the black kids."

"But that makes no sense. I was the one getting pelted with the tennis ball."

"Oh." A light seemed to click on in her mind. She pinched her eyebrows together. "You say, the black boys were throwing the ball at you?"

"Yeah."

"Well," Mae said, "in their world, white people don't let black people do that kind of thing to them. It's usually the other way around."

She must have seen my confusion because she said, "Stay right there. I pulled out the photos I told you about. They might help you understand."

She stepped into the house and returned bearing a stack of photo albums, each one the size of the Bible. She plopped them on the table and started flipping through page after page of newspaper clippings and black and white photographs. Some showed people sitting in cafés or buses. Others portrayed mobs being shot with water cannons and police wading into crowds wielding batons and wearing riot gear. One showed a policeman beating a woman with his club. Another, a dead body in a casket. It was always white officers attacking black people.

"You see?" Mae said. "It's like I told you. Black people got beat up and killed. If a black man did anything to a white man, he might find himself strung up from a tree."

"Strung up?" I asked.

"Hanged," Mae said. "Lynched."

"Oh." I didn't know what to say. How had I missed this much history?

"Let me tell you the story of Emmett Till," Mae continued. "He was a fourteen-year-old boy from Chicago visiting relatives in Mississippi when he committed the crime of speaking to a white woman. The woman's husband and brother kidnapped Emmett, beat him, killed him, and dumped his body in the river."

"Dang," I said. "Did the guys who did it go to jail?"

"No. An all-white jury acquitted them, even though the men later admitted to killing Emmett."

Mae pointed at a picture of police spraying a bunch of children with a fire hose. "I was in Birmingham," she said, "when they blew up the church and killed those four baby girls."

Just then, Mae's phone rang, and she vanished inside. I continued flipping through the pages, trying to understand this strange world I now found myself in. People picked on each other here for different reasons than in Idaho, but it was still about being different. If you were too poor, or too fat, or too thin, or too tall, or too small, or too quiet, or too loud, or too whatever, you got picked on. We didn't have any black kids in my school in Buhl, and I never saw what Mae called racism. But I couldn't understand why the color of a person's skin should matter so much. They were just people, weren't they? Maybe they spoke differently or ate different food or liked different music, but, in the end, weren't they just people? Mae was a nice old lady. Leroy was a jerk, but what did that have to do with the color of his skin? Nothing that I could see.

I finished flipping through the photo albums, but Mae hadn't returned. I stood to peer through the screen door. She sat in a poofy armchair with her head in her hands, trembling like a bowl of Jell-O. I guessed she was crying.

She sucked in her breath and let out a moan of pain that sent my heart into my mouth. Tears sprang to my eyes. I wanted to go in and wrap my arms around her big, quaking shoulders. But I couldn't do that. I was just a kid, and she was a teacher. I didn't like anyone to see me cry, and I guessed Mae wouldn't either. If she wanted me to know why she was crying, she would tell me when she was ready.

CHAPTER THIRTEEN
TALKING TO A GHOST

The police took down the yellow tape from around the park, but a piece of it still clung to the bridge. It waved at me as it fluttered in the warm breeze, inviting me into the forbidden territory. I knew I shouldn't go in. The police probably hid cameras in the trees just waiting for me to reveal myself. But I hadn't talked to Damon since they came to get him, and I had a question for him.

I sat on the bridge with my arms draped over the railing and peered up the creek into the shadows where Damon had been. It must have rained somewhere because the thin snake of water had turned into a regular stream like someone was trying to wash away the memory of Damon. I knew the stream wasn't deep because I could see a big snapper wading through it like a ship under sail.

"What happened to you?" I asked Damon's ghost. I figured it would still be hanging around the place where he died. "Did someone kill you because you were black?"

This idea seemed strange. But that's what I had seen in Mae's photos. My parents never made a big deal about the color of anyone's skin. I didn't know why it would matter. What mattered to me was how people treated me. If they were jerks, I didn't like them. But, if they were decent people, like Mae, I thought they were okay. Seemed simple. Still, I hadn't been here to experience all that history Mae had been talking about, so I wouldn't know.

WALLS OF GLASS

Anyway, I still had to figure out what to do with Damon's money. I hid it under the dresser in my room in an old shoe box, but I couldn't bring myself to spend it. Every time I tried, I knew something would go wrong. How do you explain buying a new trumpet that costs four hundred dollars when you're just a paperboy? Besides, that money wasn't mine. I needed to find out who it belonged to so I could give it back—so I could do the right thing. Maybe Damon had a wife and kids somewhere who needed his money.

I waited for Damon to say something—to give me some clue about how I could get out of the mess I had created. It's crazy how one mistake can lead to a dozen more until you're swamped in three feet of muck with no way to drain the pond.

No mystical communications came, so I gave up, climbed on my bike, and rode up to the corner market. I needed to do something mindless for a while—to escape my underdeveloped brain if only for a few minutes. I popped a quarter in the *Centipede* machine and spun the ball. Five bucks later, my wrist hurt so bad I had to quit. I bought a bunch of *Zero* candy bars and checked out the comic books.

A *Zero* candy bar is the closest thing to heaven you can place in your mouth. It's got white fudge on the outside, dark caramel, and almond and peanut nougat on the inside. I figured the candy bars had a white coating because they were simply divine. I always ate them slowly to savor the smooth sweetness. Mom said they rotted my teeth, but it was worth it. A couple of *Zero* bars could make any problem melt away in an ecstasy of flavor.

I turned to leave the store when I saw Oscar standing next to a big man with dirty cowboy boots and long hair. I slipped behind the comic aisle because I didn't need a confrontation with Oscar at the moment. Oscar's face was so flat it looked like he'd crashed into a telephone pole. Or maybe his mom had ironed it when he was little.

The man browsed the cigarettes when Oscar picked up a package of Red Man tobacco and said something to him. The man slapped Oscar upside the head, sending his baseball cap flying. He yanked the tobacco from Oscar's hand. When Oscar bent down to pick up his hat, he noticed me watching him. He glared at me as he straightened and doubled up his fist.

Oscar didn't have time to do anything because the man pushed him toward the checkout counter. When a black man stepped in front of him from a side aisle, the man with the dirty cowboy boots cursed real loud, threw his cigarettes on the counter and stomped toward the door, shoving Oscar in front of him. Oscar tried to scramble out of the way, but he didn't escape the boot that guy planted on his backside with a sound like a ninety-mile-an-hour pitch hitting a catcher's glove.

"Dimwit. Get in the car," the man sneered.

As Oscar yanked on the car door handle, our gazes met through the greasy store window. He glowered at me with so much hatred that I just stood there like an idiot, not knowing what to do.

Jeremy's mom gave me a satisfied smirk when I arrived at their house on Monday afternoon. She must have thought she was doing me a favor by letting me play with her stuck-up kid. I shrugged and escaped to the backyard where Jeremy's dad had carried his big fish tank. The tropical fish darted about in a tiny glass bowl like a twisting rainbow. Jeremy glanced up and raised a dripping net.

"I got them out for you," he said.

I surveyed the backyard just to be sure he was talking to me.

I shrugged. "We don't have any place to put a bunch of fish at my house," I said.

Somebody had given us two gerbils in a cage a few days before. Mom made us keep them because she didn't want us to be rude, but we didn't have a fish tank big enough for all those fish.

Jeremy curled his upper lip. "I'm not *giving* them to you." He smirked. "I just got them out so we can clean the tank."

Oh, of course. I should have known. The way he said "we" was the same way he said "we" could play with his *Star Wars* stuff. I had been dumb enough to let him snooker me into coming over again. This was worse than watching him play. Now the simpering jerk would watch me work.

I almost left right then, but I remembered Mom telling me not to be rude before I left our house. We dumped the tank over on the grass, and I scrubbed all the fish crap off the walls while he sprayed the rocks with the hose.

When his mom called him in for lunch, I walked right past the door. I wasn't going to sit there and listen to him eat again. And I couldn't stand seeing his mom wrinkle her nose at me like I was a bit of nasty stuff stuck to the bottom of her shoe. Jeremy could dump the stupid fish back into the tank himself.

Escaping from one scene of suffering, however, landed me right in the middle of another. I found Mom, up to her elbows in soapy water, crying at the sink. I considered asking her what happened, but it didn't seem like she wanted to talk. Instead, I searched for Clint until I found him perched up in the tree reading a comic book.

"What's wrong with Mom?" I asked.

He grunted. "Jeremy's mom." He said this like it should be all the explanation I would need. When I just stared at him, he shook his head and lowered his comic book. "I swear, if your head didn't follow your legs around, you'd lose it. Don't you pay attention to anything?"

"What?"

"That stuck-up lady has been acting like Mom's friend all while she's been going around telling mean stories about her at work."

Well, that didn't surprise me. Jeremy's mom looked like the kind of person who would be two-faced.

Clint continued. "She called the child welfare people. They came down here while you were off at that jerk's house. She complained that Katie was out in our yard in her diaper again."

What do you say to that? Was this discrimination? I didn't know, but it sure felt like it.

CHAPTER FOURTEEN
WALLS OF GLASS

You need to shadow this part here," Mrs. Took said. "Do you see it?"

She bent over me, smelling of vanilla-scented perfume. We had worked on drawing dogs and cats for a while before moving to birds. I wanted to draw something meaningful about the world like Mrs. Took encouraged us to do. My first attempt at a cardinal sitting on a branch failed. It just wouldn't work for me. I gave up and drew the image that kept invading my dreams. For some reason, this came easier. When Mrs. Took saw it, she gave me a penetrating glance before pointing to where I was messing it up.

I dragged the smudger around until it looked better.

"I can't get the wing right," I said. "It's driving me crazy."

She took my hand in hers and carefully traced the shape of the wing. Her cold hand was reassuring.

"Now, you finish it," she said. "Remember where the light is. That will help you know where to place the shadows."

It still took me a long time to get it right, but when I did, I sat back to study it. I had sketched the cardinal lying dead in the dirt with his feathers fanning out. Its beak opened a crack as if it had just given its last gasp. It wasn't perfect, but you could tell it was a cardinal.

I swallowed the guilt that rose in my throat. Killing a cardinal

WALLS OF GLASS

seemed like a sin. Nothing that beautiful should be shot down in cold blood. I thought of Damon. He looked so kind and strong in the picture they printed in the newspaper. Nobody like him should die alone the way he had.

Drawing the picture of the cardinal did something for me. I don't know how to explain it. I just felt better, like I had released something that had been trapped inside me.

Mrs. Took gazed at the drawing for a long time. Then, she peered at me over her thick-rimmed glasses. "The artist's work is always a window into his soul," she said.

It didn't take me long to realize that an evil Jedi from the Dark Side had created seventh-grade math—designed to force you to give in to anger and hatred. Math had been cool when it consisted of simple multiplication and division. I could even handle fractions. When they threw in x's and y's, my brain shriveled up.

That wasn't the worst of it though. Our math teacher, Mr. Custard, proved to be some kind of cowboy wannabe. He sported short-cropped hair and a Hitler mustache that quivered under his nose like a fluffy caterpillar. He wore black cowboy boots with wrangler jeans and a dinner-plate-sized belt buckle that was almost wider than his waist. All the kids knew he stashed booze in a desk drawer because we checked. That explained why he smelled like a brewery half the time.

He tapped the big glass jar that perched on the edge of his desk with a ruler when he wanted our attention. He had explained the jar the first day of class.

"This," he said, holding it up like one of those women selling dish soap in the TV ads, "is the bubble gum jar. If I catch you chewing gum in my class, you'll deposit the gum in the jar."

He flashed a malicious smile. His Hitler mustache trembled with delight. "And," he continued, "you will select a new piece to continue chewing."

The ticking of the clock sounded harsh in the ensuing quiet.

"He can't do that," someone whispered. But he heard her.

"Oh, yes I can. Please, someone, test me. Pleeeeease."

WALLS OF GLASS

He gazed around the room as if he hoped someone would jump up and smack their gum right in his face. But no one stirred. The sight of all that chewed up gum turned my stomach.

Well, I hadn't had much luck finding a friend my age in Stillwater, or of any age at all. I thought Mae was my friend, but she wouldn't answer her door anymore—not since the phone call. I knew because I had been back to Mae's house almost every day since she had shown me the photo albums. Twice, I tried talking to the Hispanic kid from science class, but he ignored me and joined a group of Mexican kids. I guessed we were supposed to be divided up into nice, neat categories based on our language and skin color.

I thought it strange that all of us twelve- and thirteen-year-olds struggling with our self-esteem and trying to find our place in the world simply copied the adults around us. We all crawled into the comfortable categories someone else created for us because they were easy and safe. But I could see that the walls between us were made of glass. One little crack and they would shatter. Then the whole world would see that our categories were just make-believe—lies we told ourselves so we wouldn't have to face the truth—the truth that we were all pretty much the same, ordinary people, struggling to find meaning and acceptance.

I gave up on kids at Stillwater Junior High and went looking for friends where they couldn't turn away from me. I finally found a friend one day at recess. His name was J. R. R. Tolkien. Our friendship started when I read *The Hobbit*. His words carried me out of that asphalt jungle with its simmering hostility between white and black, rich and poor, to a place where evil was clear to see and good always triumphed in the end. I knew it wasn't real, but it should have been.

Once I made his acquaintance, Tolkien introduced me to lots of new friends whose stories I followed with rapt attention. I even became jealous of them. I'm not saying I wanted to face dragons or goblins who tried to roast me alive or rip out my guts. But at least they knew who the bad guys were, and they knew how to defeat them. I don't want to say their lives seemed simple, but well, their lives seemed simple.

I peddled past Mae's house and was heading down the long sloping hill under the canopy of trees when I heard a low growl. The black and white speckled dog burst from the underbrush heading right toward me. I hesitated for a second. His flop ears whipped in the wind, and his tongue dangled out.

That crazy dog was going to attack me. I leaned over my handlebars and pumped the peddles for all I was worth. Wind rushed through my hair, making my eyes water. It caught my paper bag, filling it like a balloon. The drag made me work harder as the bottom of the hill approached. I needed all the speed I could get.

I chanced a glance back, thinking I'd outdistanced him, but he was right behind me. His teeth snapped at the paper bag, but I veered away. The white rickety fence surrounding my next house was only a few dozen yards away. If I could just make it.

My bike jerked sideways. I looked up into the green canopy overhead as my body rotated in mid-air. I landed flat on my stomach. The wind rushed out of me. I rolled in a tangle of bike and paper bags, thrashing to free myself before that stupid dog got a hold of my throat. My lungs spasmed and struggled to suck in air. I scrambled to my knees, gasping as my lungs inflated, but something heavy slammed into my side and bowled me over. I stared into the dog's eyes as he washed my face with a wet tongue. His hair tickled my nose.

"Get off."

I shoved him. He bounded away, squatted low, and then jumped on me again.

"What's the matter with you?" I shouted. "You could have killed me."

Someone whistled, and the dog jumped away. The gate slammed as I crawled to my feet while untangling myself from the paper bag.

The old man I delivered the paper to knelt on the road and rubbed the dog's head with both hands.

"He likes you," he said.

"He tried to kill me," I mumbled.

The old man smiled. "Nah. He was just playing. Dogs used to be wolves and when something runs from them, they can't help but chase it."

"I wasn't running from him. I was just riding my bike."

"Looked like you were running to me," the old man said with a grin.

I dusted off my pants and shirt and examined the new raspberry on my elbow. It oozed blood. I pulled my bike up.

"Stupid dog," I mumbled.

The old man stood, and the dog padded over to me. He looked up at me with pale blue eyes.

"I wouldn't be so quick to dismiss a friend," the old man said. "Friends are hard to come by."

I bowed my head. It was true, but a dog that did nothing but cause trouble wasn't much of a friend. Maybe he was the only friend I would ever have here. I pushed my bike while I walked off the pain in my knee. Then I mounted it and rode away. The dog trotted behind me until I was almost home before he took off after a rabbit. Friends *were* hard to come by in Oklahoma. That was true enough. And just as easily lost.

Weeks bled into one another as I slogged through my classes and wrestled with the terrifying temptation of Damon's money and what to do with it. The wretched heat gave way to cool evenings. Sycamore trees shook their leaves to the ground. Insects went to sleep, and Halloween arrived. But Halloween was a letdown. I was too old to dress up for trick-or-treating this year, and the school didn't put on a spook alley like the one in Buhl, Idaho did.

Mr. Sentury came to school dressed as a mummy on Halloween. He didn't wear shorts anymore because it was too cold out, but he still ran his nose up his arm. The wet streak glistened on the white cloth he had wrapped around his arms.

"Now," he said, "today we will mummify Mindi. If you would come up here please."

Mindi gave an exaggerated sigh and walked to the front of the class. We all knew the routine by now. People liked to complain, but secretly we all enjoyed it.

"Lie down on the table," he said.

"You will recall," he continued, "from our last section on ancient Egypt, that the practice of mummification was restricted to the upper class for most of Egyptian history. Because the Egyptians believed the spirit would die if the body was not preserved, those who could afford it made sure they were embalmed so their spirits would live on. Most people couldn't afford the expense of embalming and building a tomb filled with food and servants for the afterlife, which meant that only the very wealthy, like the Pharaohs, could live forever."

When he launched into a description of the mummification process, I quit listening. Why did money even matter in religion? Why did money matter at all? Weren't my parents just as good as people that lived in the big houses on the other side of town? When Mr. Sentury pointed to the row of jars he stacked up on the little bookcase, I paid attention again.

"Come forward class," he said with a wave of his bandaged hand. "We'll remove her internal organs and preserve them in honey so she can be happy in the afterlife."

"Honey?" someone asked as we shuffled to the front of the room to surround the table where Mindi lay.

Mr. Sentury glared at the class. "If I said honey, I meant honey," he said. "Don't tell me you don't know that honey never goes bad."

"Yes, it does," one of the black kids said. "I have a whole jar at home that's hard as a rock."

Mr. Sentury gave him a simpering smile.

"It's not bad," he said. "All you have to do is heat it up, and it will turn back to liquid. Even the ancient Egyptians knew this." He rubbed his chin with his thumb. "And since it's Halloween, I have an instructive story for you."

We all waited. Mr. Sentury could be weird, but he was interesting.

"Once," he began in a mysterious voice, "some tomb robbers broke into an Egyptian tomb deep beneath the desert sand. They found jars filled with honey. When they sat down to eat their lunch, they dipped their bread into the honey and found it was still perfectly good. Even after 3,000 years."

"So?" someone said.

"So," Mr. Sentury continued with an elevated eyebrow, "one of them noticed a long, black hair on his bread. He lifted a candle and peered into the jar. What do you think he saw?"

We all exchanged nervous glances.

"A liver?" someone said.

Mr. Sentury shook his head. "A mummified baby."

A few girls shrieked. The boys just blinked they were so shell-shocked. I gave a nervous laugh and vowed I would never eat another drop of honey again.

"You see," he continued, "honey can last forever, and it's a great preservative. Now, let's rip out Mindi's organs. Who has the long hook?"

"What for?" Mindi said, her eyes widening.

I guess the story about the hair freaked her out the most since she was the one being mummified.

"To pull your brains out your nose, of course," Mr. Sentury said.

"That's it." Mindi sat bolt upright, swung her legs around, and hopped off the table. "I'm out of here." One of the girls started crying. Another asked to be excused.

Mr. Sentury sent more kids to the office with nervous fits than any teacher in the history of teaching. I came away with a different lesson from the class that day than I think Mr. Sentury intended. It seemed obvious that certain people had special privileges, even today. I wasn't sure the privileges only came with wealth either. Skin color seemed to be part of the equation in a way I was just now beginning to understand. Still, why didn't the Egyptian peasants get to be buried with all the food and fixings for a feast in the afterlife? Who produced all that food anyway? Not the rich. Why did the rich get to enjoy in death what they had already been privileged to enjoy in life? If the afterworld was just a reflection of the real world, then what was the point in wanting to go there? If things didn't get better for you, why bother?

After dinner that night, I led my little brothers and sister around to trick-or-treat. That year, rumors flew that some lunatics were sticking sharp objects into Halloween candy. Mom insisted that we only go to the houses of people we knew, which didn't take long.

Of course, I didn't take them to Jeremy's house, but he came to ours. I couldn't believe he would be such a bald-faced pig he would beg candy from a family his own mother had tried to ruin. I still had a lot to learn about discrimination.

The black and white speckled dog found us and followed us home. My little brother tried to drag him into the house, but he wouldn't come in. When the dog broke free, he bounded to the edge of the yard and barked at us. I guess he wasn't an inside dog.

CHAPTER FIFTEEN
WINDOW TO THE SOUL

I t's about that time in the semester," Mrs. Took said, "when you're all prepared to start creating real art. True art is not simply a nice drawing."

She raised her glasses to the top of her head with a jingle of bracelets.

"It communicates something deep down about who you are. I want you to take the next week and create a work of art in any of the mediums we've explored. Create from your hearts. Find the beauty, the sorrow, the anger, or the hope from within, and give it expression in your art."

I took her seriously. The only medium I had been able to do at all was the pencil and paper. I couldn't paint because I didn't understand colors. Not at all. Every time I tried to mix colors, they came out wrong.

I picked up my pencils, my eraser, and my smudgers, and retreated to the corner that had become mine. The window there overlooked the asphalt playground. I gazed through the dirty glass. The swing swayed back and forth. It seemed so forlorn and lonely—like it longed for companionship in a wide, barren world that had forgotten it. That was an emotion I understood—an emotion I thought Damon would have understood.

I closed my eyes, thought for a moment, and drew a picture about me.

Mr. Custard made two kids who forgot to spit the gum out of their mouths before class pick a new piece out of the jar. The boy threw up in the trash can. The girl smacked the gum real loud and made jokes about it.

During the math test, one of the popular white kids that sat behind me kept trying to see over my shoulder. I'd seen his mother drop him off that morning in a purple Corvette. He tapped me with his pencil so often I turned around and whispered, "Leave me alone."

Mr. Custard scowled and called me to the front of the room.

"To the hall, Jim."

"My name is James," I said.

"That will be another one for sassing."

"I wasn't cheating," I said. "He was trying to cheat off of me."

Mr. Custard curled his lip in disgust. "If I had a penny for every time some lazy student has tried that excuse, I'd be as rich as the King of Persia. Now get out in the hallway."

I slouched out and grabbed my ankles. Boy, did he pack a wallop. For someone so thin and frail looking, he sure could make that paddle sing.

The rich kid, who had been trying to cheat, caught me at lunch recess. He shoved me so hard that I stumbled backward. My Tolkien books and pencil drawings spilled across the black asphalt.

"Tattletale," he said. "You tried to get me in trouble."

"You shouldn't cheat," I said.

I should have kept my mouth shut, but he made angry. That jerk got me spanked. A crowd gathered the way they did when the white kid and the black girl fought. It really was sick how they crowded around us like a pack of hyenas salivating over a kill. My mouth went dry, and I felt weak all over.

Clint's advice kept running through my brain like a stuck record. "If he hits me, I have to hit him back. If he hits me, I have to hit him back." I knew Clint would kill me if I didn't. He might even throw me out of the family.

The kid grabbed my shirt and pushed me. I had spent six months studying Judo back in Idaho. It wasn't much, but I knew to push back enough to get him to commit to pushing harder so I could use his own strength against him.

"I'm gonna teach the new boy he can't tattletale around here," he said announced to the crowd.

I saw from his expression that he planned to use his height and weight advantage to shove me down, sit on my chest, and beat me to a pulp. So I did the only thing I could do.

I waited until he leaned into me with all his weight. Then I fell backward, planting my foot on his belly. As I rolled, I kicked out hard, sending him sailing over my head. He landed with a thump and a rush of air as he hit the asphalt. I rolled to my knees to find him lying motionless. He wasn't even breathing. I worried I had killed him.

Then one of his friends rushed over to him. The boy raised a hand and gasped for breath. His friend dragged him to his feet. The kid never even looked at me. He just stumbled back into the school.

The silent crowd watched me crawl to my feet, trembling like a leaf in a hurricane. I don't know what they thought or what they expected. I picked up my things. Then someone started clapping. My face flushed, and I pushed my way through the crowd. A few people patted me on the back before I could escape.

Damon no longer drew me to the park. He wasn't there to listen anymore. But he continued to haunt me. That wad of bills I kept hidden under my dresser nagged at me like an ingrown toenail. I longed to get rid of it. But I didn't know how. Throwing the whole wad into the ditch seemed like such a waste. I considered mailing it to the police like I had the wallet, but I worried if I used the same typewriter, they would figure out who I was. Instead, I kept it tucked away in the little cardboard box under the dresser. With Damon gone and Mae ignoring me, I settled into a routine of going to school and delivering my papers.

Now and then, I would pull the box out and count the bills, just to feel them slip through my fingers, wishing I could figure out a way to spend it without anyone knowing. I didn't need it for video games and comic books. My paper route money gave me plenty for that. I wanted something big, like a new bike or a new trumpet. What was the point of having a lot of money if you couldn't buy something big?

I hadn't seen Mae since that day in September when I left her crying. The weeds had taken over her front yard again, so I figured I should mow it for her. When I knocked on her door to see if she wanted me to cut the weeds, she never answered. I knew she was home because her car was in the driveway, and I could hear the radio playing. It always blared out sappy love songs from the 50s and 60s. I couldn't see why she liked that kind of music, but I guess you never outgrow the music you grow up with.

Once or twice, I saw police cars out front. I never found out what they were doing because when I saw the police, I always gave them a wide berth. They might have one of those police dogs that could just sniff out a criminal from miles away. I didn't want them taking an interest in me, so I just gave up trying to see Mae.

The black and white dog found me sometimes, and we raced down the hill past the white picket fence. He nipped at my heels as I peddled but never tried to drag me off the bike. When we got close to my house, he'd wander off.

"What do you want to do when you grow up?" Mrs. Took asked me while she was showing me how to position the lines and use shading on my new picture. I visited her room during lunch one day to get help with my drawings. But I kept going back because it was the only safe place in the entire school. No one chucked tennis balls at my head or tried to beat me up in her room.

I shrugged. "I don't know," I said. "I kind of wanted to be an archaeologist or a historian, I guess."

"Really," she said. "I had you pegged for a lawyer."

I glanced up at her. Was she serious? She smiled at my expression.

"You have empathy," she said. She pointed to my drawing. "Look at this. Why would you draw a picture of a boy sitting alone on a

WALLS OF GLASS

swing with his head down in an empty playground? I don't know if you meant to do it, but you've captured a deep sadness in this picture. One that every human heart has felt."

Well, this was news to me. I was just trying to draw a picture of me at recess. I wasn't sad—at least I didn't think I was.

"It's just a drawing," I said.

Mrs. Took lifted her glasses to the top of her head. Her gaze bored into me like she was reading my soul.

"I don't think you know who you are yet, James." She poked a finger at my chest. "There's someone in there that wants to be let out."

Well, that was just creepy. I glanced down at my chest, waiting for some alien to rip it open, stick its head out and say, "What's for lunch?"

She smiled again. "I'm speaking metaphorically." Like I was supposed to know what "metaphorically" meant.

"It's just a figure of speech," she said. "It means you're discovering who you're going to be. Everybody goes through this."

"Really?"

I didn't think Clint had any trouble with this. He knew who he was. He always had the answers. I knew I was a knucklehead who was hiding a dead man's cash, and who was too afraid to spend it. I didn't know what else I might be.

CHAPTER SIXTEEN
OF PINK AND PICKLES

One of the new gerbils Mom's friend gave us had an evil, pink eye that watched my every move. The cage sat on our dresser, giving her a good view of me no matter where I was in the room. It was creepy. She twitched her snout and blinked that eye like she had a nervous tic, the way insane people always had on TV shows.

She wanted out of that cage like nobody's business. While the other gerbil jogged in the squeaky wheel, this one made a nest in one corner and piled everything she could on top of it. She climbed up on the pile and stretched her fingers for the top of the cage, so I slammed a big book on it, just in case. We had enough mice running around the house. The last thing I wanted was some pink-eyed devil nibbling on my toes.

Clint didn't like the gerbils any more than I did, and he refused to care for them. By Saturday, the nasty rat smell of their dirty cage became unbearable, and I decided to clean it. The pink-eyed devil backed away from my hand while snapping her jaws and hissing. I put on a pair of gloves to avoid those sharp teeth and smashed her up against the bars with one hand and grabbed her by the tail with the other. When I lifted her up, her tail slid off the bone.

She hit the bottom of the cage and freaked out. While she did somersaults, I gaped at the furry tail dangling from my fingers. Had I just made a lifelong enemy? I didn't stick my hand back in there to grab her again because I figured she would scramble up my arm and rip my eyes out with those sharp teeth.

Instead, I grabbed a plastic cup from the kitchen and scooped her up in it. I dumped her in a clear plastic tub with the other gerbil and dropped a dictionary on top to keep them inside. She glared at me with that twitching, pink eye while I cleaned the cage with soap and water.

While the cage dried, I dragged the lawn mower to Mae's house since I couldn't break into her garage to get hers. I'd been thinking about her weed patch for days. It's like I owned it now that I had mowed it twice. Besides, I felt sorry for her. She was an old lady with a bad leg, and she needed help.

It had been dry lately, so the weeds weren't as tough as they were the first two times I had mowed. I was finishing up when pain stabbed into my leg—like a knife jabbing in all the way to the bone. I howled and hopped away from the lawn mower. For a second, I thought the big, black snake had slithered up behind me and sunk its fangs into my leg.

The mower coughed and sputtered to a stop. The angry buzz of a thousand wasps filled the air like the roar of some beast with a million voices. They poured out of a hole in the ground the size of a golf ball that lay hidden underneath a clump of dead weeds left over from the last time I mowed. It was like the entire fleet of Imperial TIE fighters swarmed out of the Death Star to hunt me down. Another one got me on the arm before I jumped into action.

I slapped at it and yanked the cord on the mower. It roared to life. I jerked it over the hole, taking fiendish delight in the thought of all those nasty wasps getting chopped to pieces. I waited a few minutes before I pulled the mower away. They flooded out again, so I shoved the mower back over the hole. Now, what could I do? The blades weren't killing them at all. The wind just blew them back down their hole.

If I let the mower die, they would swarm me, chew me to bits, and drag my pieces down into their little dungeon to eat me slowly. Another one of the escapees found me. It stung me right on the top of the head. I slapped at it without thinking. It latched itself to my hand, stinging everywhere it could reach. I screamed again and let the mower die. Another found my cheek. Then another latched onto my ear. A high, girly scream of terror that could have shattered glass ripped from my throat.

Something hit me on the back. I spun around, wild-eyed, expecting to see a queen wasp the size of dog fly up to stab me to the heart with her spear-like stinger. But Mae stood on the porch, waving frantically.

I gave my hand a mighty shake as I sprinted for the porch. Mae ushered me through the door and slammed it as a dozen wasps bounced off the screen. They buzzed, angrily searching the entire screen for a way in. The house smelled of mold and mothballs. It was so strong I could taste it on my tongue.

Mae jammed her hands onto her ample hips and gave me a disbelieving smirk. "Boy, you've got a death wish," she said. "First, it's a cottonmouth. Then, it's a nest of the biggest wasps in Payne County." She shook her head. "Come into the kitchen."

Pain County was right, because I sure kept finding an awful lot of pain down here. I glanced at my hand, which was already swelling around the red puncture wounds. Mae pulled a jar of pickles out of the fridge and cut them into round slices. This surprised me because I hoped she had some kind of medicine to take the sting away, but she seemed to think I was hungry.

"You don't seem allergic to them," she said.

"I don't think so," I said.

"Nah, you'd be as big as a rhino by now and struggling to breathe after all those stings."

"It still hurts," I said.

Maybe if I stated the obvious, she would get the hint. I didn't want her thinking all I needed were a few slices of pickle.

"Sit down," she said. "Let me see that hand."

I raised it to her.

"Mercy," she said. "You couldn't just get stung once, could you?"

She piled a bunch of cold dill pickles over the angry red welts on my hand.

"Um, do you have any medicine?" I asked. My mom was a nurse, after all. I didn't know what it would do to her to see her own son come home doctored with pickles.

Mae smiled. I hadn't seen her smile much. She had a lingering beauty when she did. She must have turned a lot of heads when she was younger.

"Give it a minute," she said as she wrapped a cloth bandage around my hand. "Did they get you anywhere else?"

I told her, and she tied slices of pickle to my arm and my ankle. Then she made me hold the cold, wet pickle slices to my cheek and ear while she held one on my head. She tied them all on with a big strip of white cloth. Soon, all I could smell was the strong, vinegary odor of pickles.

All wrapped up in pickles, I knew I looked like one of those dead guys in the movies who had to have their mouths tied shut. All I needed were the gold coins on my eyes. Mae hid another smile behind her hand.

By the time she finished with my head, my hand already felt better.

"Thanks," I said.

She waved me away. "I should be thanking you for tackling that weed patch again."

We sat in uncomfortable silence for a while. I wanted to ask her about the police cars and that phone call, but I didn't want to make her mad. Something I did last time I was here flipping through her photo albums had offended her. She had been ignoring me for weeks.

"I'm sorry I haven't been answering the door," she said.

I studied my shoes.

"I've been sick lately."

"It's okay," I said.

I wondered about her bad leg, but I didn't want to hear what had been ailing her. She was an old lady. Her list of ailments must have been a mile long. I wouldn't understand what any of them were anyway, so I figured I should bring the discussion back to the problem at hand.

"How am I going to get the lawn mower off that hole?" I asked.

Mae shook her head. "Boy, I have a feeling you and trouble must be real good friends."

"That's about the size of it," I said. "It's my brain. It doesn't work right."

Now Mae laughed, and her belly shook. "I never knew a boy your age whose brain *did* work right," she said. She gave a great big sigh. "Lordy, child, you are a character."

I didn't know why what I said was funny. I was just telling her the truth.

Mae patted her belly and shook her head. "I guess you'll have to move real fast," she said.

Sitting around in the kitchen with pickles strapped to my head wasn't going to solve the problem. I stood up and wandered into the front room, thinking I might find some inspiration if I studied the situation through the screen door for a while. That's when I saw her.

The picture I found in Damon's wallet of the chubby dark-skinned baby with the pink bow in her hair sat on the mantelpiece. Beside it, smiling down at me like Jacob Marley's ghost in the story *A Christmas Carol*, was the picture of an African man with a caption that read, "In Memory of Damon Wiggins."

I froze. The blood pounded in my head and pushed against my eyes so hard I expected them to pop out and shoot across the room. I spun to face Mae. She frowned at my wild expression. I spun back to the photo of Damon.

"You miserable, little thief," Damon said inside my brain. "You'll never leave until I get my money back."

That's when I bolted. I slammed through the screen door, missing all the steps as I flew to the lawn mower. I snagged the handle with one hand and yanked it after me. It bounced and tried to turn over, but I was flying so fast that no nasty wasps could catch me—and neither could Damon's ghost.

The shock of seeing Damon's photo on Mae's mantel froze all the cells in my brain. All the way home, not one complete thought managed to work its way through my thick skull. It screeched to a halt and froze on the image of Damon's face, searing it forever into my memory.

I had been running away from the problems I had caused. But Damon would live forever in my mind. Until I found the courage to do the right thing, I would never be free. I knew Mae would never speak to me again once she found out what I had done. She might even throw me in jail. But I had to give Mae Damon's money. It was hers. I had no right to it. Not even the ancient law of "finders keepers, losers weepers" could justify my actions anymore.

CHAPTER SEVENTEEN
THE NEW GIRL

I barely noticed that I had walked into our front room until Dawn took one look at me and burst out laughing.

"Nice get up," Clint said. "You do know Halloween is over? If you're trying to be a mummy, you'll have to use more wrappings."

"What?" I said.

"You smell like you took a bath in a pickle jar," my little brother said.

I patted my head and felt the bulge of the pickles under the wrappings. I had forgotten about Mae's pickle wraps. I had dragged the mower all the way home looking like this. No wonder people crossed the street to avoid me.

When I yanked the wrappings off, Dawn grabbed her belly and doubled over, convulsing with laughter. She fell to her knees, weeping, and wringing her hands.

Clint shook his head and gave me a wry smile. "Been throwing rocks at wasp nests again, huh?"

We had done that once in a park only to be chased by a swarm of angry wasps. That time I got off easy, but they got Clint good. I glanced down at my swollen hand and then reached up to feel my cheek and ear. My cheek was the size of a baseball, and my ear felt like someone had stuffed a boulder into my ear lobe. I must have looked like some Martian reject on steroids or a Frankenstein

WALLS OF GLASS

experiment gone wrong.

Mom came in, drawn by Dawn's guffaws. "Land sakes!" she said when she saw me standing there all swollen with bandages dangling from my hands and smelling of pickles. "What have you gotten into now?"

"Wasps," I said. "Mae put pickles on them."

Clint and Dawn both burst out in a chorus of laughter.

Mom's brow furrowed. "Who's Mae?"

"A lady on my paper route."

Mom shook her head. "Why use folk remedies when you can take Benadryl?" she mumbled.

"It worked," I said. The pain had gone down, but not the swelling.

Mom gestured to Clint and Dawn. "Get out of here you two and leave him alone."

My baby sister came in as I swallowed the Benadryl. She took one look at me and started crying. I retreated to my room.

The first thing I saw was the mouse-size hole in the plastic tub where I left the gerbils. A neat pile of plastic shavings sat beside the hole like the little jerk had planned the whole thing. I glanced at the cage, but it was empty.

"Oh no," I yelled. "You've got to be kidding."

This brought my entire family to crowd into my room. I suppose they hoped for more entertainment at my expense, but Mom turned all white when she found out about the missing gerbils and forced us to search the entire house. I checked under the dresser because I didn't want anyone else finding my box full of money, but the gerbils were gone—escaped. We now had two fugitive gerbils on the loose, and one of them was gunning for me because I had ripped off her tail.

"They've probably joined all those mice under the house," Clint said.

I imagined that pink-eyed devil gathering all the mice together in some dank cavern deep beneath our house and organizing them for war. She was going to create a huge army full of mice whose relatives I had killed, and they were coming for me. Heck, they might even overrun the entire city like that army of Stormtroopers in *Star Wars*.

That night, Clint clicked on the big box fan to circulate the stuffy air in our room. Even over the fan, I was sure I could hear the scratching of millions of tiny mice feet marching up to carry me away to their mouse dungeon for judgment.

The Benadryl must have been working because somehow I drifted off to sleep only to find Damon laughing at me and shaking a jar filled with wasps the size of mice. "They're coming for you," he laughed.

Then the pink-eyed gerbil came running toward me swinging a sword the size of a toothpick. "He's mine," she cried, flashing her jagged teeth.

Damon twisted the lid off the jar with a wicked grin. Mice-sized wasps launched themselves at my head as the mouse army grabbed my feet. They started a tug-of-war while I dangled between them shrieking in terror.

"I found your stupid gerbil," Clint said the next morning as he picked up the fan and gave it a shake.

A bloody ball of fur flopped onto the carpet. It oozed into a furry puddle.

"He's not my gerbil," I said. "I never wanted him."

"Looks like he got his block knocked off," Clint said. "Serves him right for trying to run through a fan."

"That's not the monster," I said.

Clint cast me a sharp glance. "What?"

"The one with the pink eye. She's out to get me."

Clint shook his head. "Sometimes I think you really are brain damaged."

"I pulled her tail off," I blurted. I was desperate to get him to understand the gravity of the situation.

"What did you do that for?"

"It just slipped off."

Clint nodded and assumed a serious, business-like demeanor. "Yep, you're a goner," he said. Then he slapped me on the back. I winced.

"Don't worry. I'll bury what's left of you when she's done."

WALLS OF GLASS

The gerbil escape gave me temporary amnesia about Mae, Damon, and their money. But after I dumped the squished gerbil into the trash can and everyone else wandered away to watch Saturday cartoons, I decided to pull out the money and devise a plan for getting it back to Mae without her knowing what I had done.

I blocked the door to my room and reached under the dresser for Damon's money. At least now I knew what I needed to do with it. The question was how? I swept my hand around until I could snatch the little box that held the money. I popped the lid off and dropped the box.

The pink-eyed devil sprang out at me, snapping her teeth as if she wanted to sink them into my throat. I gave her a good kick that sent her skidding across the floor. She scrambled to her feet. Our gazes met. Her whiskers twitched, and she launched herself under the bed and disappeared.

Only then did I glance down at Damon's money. Bills scattered everywhere. Right in the middle was a tangled pile of chewed up one hundred-dollar bills. I sank to my knees. Despair washed over me, clutching at my heart. I let the mangled bills slip through my fingers.

This was the pink-eyed devil's revenge—maybe the revenge of every mouse I had ever killed. Just when I discovered who the money belonged to, the demon gerbil tried to destroy me. I couldn't hand Mae a giant gerbil's nest. What would she do? The police would never believe me if I told them the gerbil ate it. That's like telling your teacher the dog ate your homework. Everyone would think it was a lie.

With trembling hands, I counted the remaining bills. That stupid gerbil had eaten six one hundred-dollar bills. Six hundred dollars! Tears welled up in my eyes and spilled onto the money. Now that I knew what to do with the money, I couldn't do it. Every time I tried to do the right thing something went wrong. I was cursed. Cursed with the worst luck of any kid in the history of the world.

I gathered my strength, found an empty glass canning jar, and stuffed the remaining bills inside. It had been stupid to leave the money in my room anyway, because anyone could have found it. I screwed the lid on as tight as I could. Then I carried it outside and buried it under the sycamore tree in the backyard. I wasn't taking any more chances.

The next morning, Mom eyeballed my still-swollen face and shook her head. "You can't go to school looking like that," she said.

The Benadryl had been working, but I still had a lopsided face and a club for a hand. Besides, the medicine made me so sleepy I drooled and staggered around every time Mom gave it to me. She sent me back to bed.

When I returned to school on Wednesday, there was a new girl in my history class. She had really dark skin and bushy, black hair. She wore a pink dress and had light blue eyes that glowed against her dark skin. I thought she was pretty, but that's not the kind of thing you say to a strange new girl on her first day at your school.

Mr. Sentury started murdering someone again, and I could see her getting nervous. I stepped up to her as we filed to the front of the room to take part in the execution. Even though she was a black girl, I figured she had less history around here than I did, and I wasn't going to step into some deadly love triangle by talking to her. I also knew what it was like to be ignored because you were new.

"He does this all the time," I said. "I got crushed by a mammoth the first day of school."

She stared at me like she expected my skin to peel off.

"It's okay," I said. "He's weird, but he never hurts anyone." I held out my hand. "My name's James."

She shook it. Her hand was cold and smooth. She smelled like coconuts.

"I'm Belinda."

"I'm from Idaho. Where are you from?"

"Alabama."

Someone bumped into me, and I grabbed the desk to keep from falling on top of her. I twisted around to find one of Leroy's friends sneering at me.

"You stop talking to that nigger girl," he said.

I scowled, shocked and confused by his use of the N-word. I mean, he was black. Why would he use a nasty word like that to refer to somebody he didn't even know? My family never used that word. I couldn't remember the last time I'd heard anybody use it. I tried to decide if Clint would expect me to punch him for it, but I didn't get the chance.

Belinda cocked back her hand and slapped him across the face. The slap rang high above the clamor of the students. The room fell silent as everyone spun to see what had happened.

"Yes, James?" Mr. Sentury glared at me. He passed his arm up his nose.

"I didn't do anything," I replied.

"He called me the N-word," Belinda said, pointing at the other kid.

The boy sneered at her. "You're so black you're purple," he whispered. "You're gonna regret this."

"Foul language, Michael?" Mr. Sentury said. Then he pointed to the metal file cabinet. "I won't have language like that used in my classroom."

We all knew what that meant. Michael stalked up to the cabinet, squared his shoulders, took a deep breath, and punched the cabinet as hard as he could with a loud bang. Mr. Sentury inspected it for the knuckle prints and nodded. Michael backed away, flexing his hand. He tried to act like it didn't hurt, but I knew it did.

"You too, James."

"What? I didn't do anything." How was this fair? I had already been spanked for cheating when I hadn't.

"He didn't." Belinda tried to back me up.

"James!" Mr. Sentury pointed to the cabinet.

What could I do? I stepped up to the cabinet and punched it. I punched it so hard my hand went numb for a second. Then the stab of pain sent tears springing to my eyes. I blinked fast and breathed deep. The last thing I needed to do was cry when Michael stood there smirking at me. Mr. Sentury was shaking his head.

"No dents," he said. "Again."

This time I made sure I left my knuckle prints in that cabinet because I knew I couldn't hit it again without crying.

As I stood there holding my crushed and swelling knuckles, I gazed up toward heaven.

Why? Why did I get punished every time I tried to help someone—every time I tried to do the right thing? Snakes and wasps, gerbils and file cabinets. Maybe I should stop trying.

CHAPTER EIGHTEEN
REFLECTIONS

The next time I saw Belinda, she stood with her back to the wall and the same black girl that always fought the white boy prepared to lay into her. Belinda was about the same size as the other girl. I thought she should've been scared because I'd've been, but she didn't look it. Her eyes narrowed. Her nostrils flared. Her hands balled into fists. Man, she looked scary. The other black girl swung, Belinda ducked and punched the girl right in the gut. That's when I dashed away to find the principal.

By the time we got back, they were really going at it. To my surprise, Belinda had the other girl down in a headlock and was whaling on her with the other fist. The principal waded through the sea of bloodthirsty seventh graders who cheered like spectators at a Roman Circus. He yanked the two girls apart. The black girl kept screaming the N-word while she spat up blood.

"Who started it?" The principal had to yell over her.

Belinda didn't say anything. She stood there panting, looking like some majestic African warrior queen. I was jealous—maybe even ashamed. Here I had been keeping my head down and avoiding confrontations, while Belinda had already taken on two school bullies and lived to tell the tale—and it was only her first day. At this rate, she could fight every kid in school before the end of the year.

The principal glanced at Belinda, who stood with her hands at her sides still balled into fists, breathing hard, and then at the girl who struggled to tear free from his grip. He must have made a decision because he marched that girl back into the building. With all the fights she got into, I figured he had a long history to draw on in making his decision. Now that the bloodletting was over, the thirsty crowd dispersed. I bent to help Belinda pick up her books.

"Are you okay?" I asked.

Belinda glanced at me. I could see she had a bloody lip.

"Leave me alone," she said.

Well, I thought that was rich coming from her. I was the one who had been forced to punch a file cabinet because I was talking to her. I was the one who ran for the principal to save her life—even though, as it turned out, she didn't need saving.

"Look," I said. "Mrs. Took, the art teacher, lets kids go to her room at lunch. It's a safe place if you don't want to stay out here."

She ignored me, so I withdrew to the swings to see if Tolkien had any new friends for me to meet. I wasn't doing too well finding any in Stillwater.

Damon's money dominated my thoughts. I couldn't spend it. I couldn't take it to the police, and I couldn't give it to Mae with six hundred dollars missing. What I needed was more money, and I needed it fast. But I was a paperboy who only earned about one hundred fifty dollars a month. I couldn't wait four whole months to give that money to Mae.

Maybe I could rob a bank. After all, I was already a criminal. Somehow, I didn't think anyone would hand over their money to a twelve-year-old because he pointed a BB gun at them. What if the bank guard panicked and shot me with a real gun? Who could I get to drive the get-away car? I could barely see over the steering wheel, and I didn't know how to drive. Besides, I wasn't sure the puke mobile would even start, let alone outrun the cops.

There was nothing for it. I had to get another paper route. I did, only this one had to be delivered by 6:00 a.m. Getting up at 5:00 a.m. wasn't anything unusual for me since I had been doing it in Buhl since I was ten. But I wasn't used to it anymore. I fell asleep in science and received another spanking for it from Mr. Ward.

This made me grumpy, so when Mr. Sentury started praising the Spartans, I couldn't keep my mouth shut. He told us all about the Helots and how the Spartans had enslaved the entire population and wouldn't let them carry weapons or own property. Then he told us how the Spartans lived in barracks, and the men didn't do anything but train for war because they were so scared of the Helots.

Sounded like a seriously stupid society. But I guess we weren't much different. We had enslaved Africans and Indians, and now, instead of enslaving people, we made sure those who didn't have as much as other people or who had different colored skin never forgot we didn't like them. Never forgot they didn't measure up. I had seen it here already—Jeffery and his mom and the white and black crowds at school. They all seemed to be acting just like the Spartans.

What annoyed me was the way Mr. Sentury seemed to think the Spartans were something special. He talked about them the way you would your favorite football team. When he explained how at the battle of Thermopylae, three hundred Spartans fought the entire Persian army to a standstill, I raised my hand.

"James?" he said.

"But they lost, Mr. Sentury," I said.

He raised his eyebrows and cocked his head.

I continued. "I mean, if they were so great, wouldn't they have figured out that enslaving most of the population and not allowing them to help fight their wars was a stupid idea?"

This seemed obvious.

"They lost because they were stupid," I continued. "If they had freed the Helots and stopped killing the babies they thought were deficient, they would've had a bigger population to fight the Persians, right?"

Mr. Sentury frowned. "What are you trying to say?"

I shrugged. "Seems to me they were just a bunch of racists who let their greed for money and power go to their heads. They lost to Athens because their racist society was so weak."

Mr. Sentury nodded.

I saw Belinda peering at me like she was thinking about what I said. But I didn't return her gaze. I was still mad at her.

"You could put it that way," he said. "But they were recognized as one of the greatest military powers of the era. How do you explain that?"

"Well, their men didn't have to do anything but fight, so sure, they could get good at what they did. But since they had to keep most of their army at home to keep the Helots from revolting, they couldn't do much with their military power, could they?"

Mr. Sentury nodded. "That's precisely the argument that some have used to explain why the South lost the Civil War," he said.

"We won that war," someone shouted.

One of Oscar's white friends was glaring at me. He had a butch-cut like Oscar and wore a white T-shirt.

Mr. Sentury sighed. "Wishful thinking, Kyle. If the South had won, we would have two countries instead of one, wouldn't we?" Mr. Sentury swung his ruler like a saber. "Still, as many southern-ers are quick to point out, the North wasn't exactly innocent in the slave trade. Northern financiers made big money off the trade, and the Union states of Kentucky, Missouri, Delaware, and Maryland were exempt from the 1863 Proclamation that freed the slaves in the south even though they were all slave-holding states with around 500,000 slaves."

Kyle glared at me, and I knew I was digging myself a nice-sized grave. So I kept my mouth shut. I didn't bother going to the cafe-teria at lunch. Oscar and Kyle would be waiting for me. Instead, I made a beeline for Mrs. Took's room. If they wanted me, they were going to have to work to find me.

Mrs. Took had been teaching us how to draw reflections. I strug-gled with it—a lot. I tried doing a reflection of a swan on water, but I wasn't getting the hang of it. That morning I had a different idea, and I wanted her help.

Her bracelets jingled as she came up to me. "You're early," she said.

I shrugged and flopped down in a chair. What kid wants to ad-mit to his teacher that he's hiding from the white kids who wanted to shove his face into the asphalt?

"I want to try a different picture," I said. "One of me looking into a mirror."

She nodded with a little frown. "That's pretty advanced drawing," she said. Then she gave an exaggerated shrug. "But, what the heck. You only live once."

She brought out some mirrors and set them up so I could see the back of my head in one mirror and my face in the other. Then she showed me how to draw the lines and use light and shadows to create a sense of depth to make the face look realistic.

We were still working on it when I heard shuffling at the door. I jerked around thinking the whole pack of white kids had come for me, but it was Belinda.

She gave me a nervous little smile. "Hey," she said with a lift of her hand.

Mrs. Took glanced up and smiled. "It's Belinda, right?" she asked. Belinda nodded.

"Come on in, we're working on reflections."

I didn't say anything to Belinda because I hadn't forgotten how rude she had been after I tried to help her. She sat with her hands folded in her lap and watched while I struggled over the picture. No one but Mrs. Took had ever watched me draw before, and I found that my fingers didn't want to work right. I kept smudging things wrong and having to erase a lot more than usual. I was sure Belinda thought I was some joke of an artist. The bell rang, and we got up to go to class.

"That's really good," Belinda said. "I wish I could draw."

I stared at her, sure she was mocking me, but she seemed to be serious.

"Thanks," I said.

I wanted to ignore her, but, in my life, friends were scarce.

CHAPTER NINETEEN
THE BRIDGE OF SORROW

That evening, I came across Belinda down by the creek. I hit the brakes and skidded to a stop.

She glanced over at me as I let my bike fall to the dirt. I strolled over to sit beside her. Some river birch trees, with their flaky bark peeling off, clustered around the creek, casting shade over a patch of grass that was actually green.

"You live down here?" I asked.

She jerked her head back up the road. "In the little white house," she said. Her hair was even bushier than it had been at school, and she had a big hair pick stuck in it.

I craned my neck around and frowned. "But that's Mae's house," I said.

Now she gave me that look girls like to give boys when they think they're being stupid. I don't know if it's true, but girls always seem to think boys have pea-sized brains that aren't good for much.

"I know whose house it is," she said.

"But Mae lives by herself. I know her."

Belinda raised her eyebrows at me and smirked. "Oh, you know everything about her, do you?"

"Well, no, but—"

"I'm her granddaughter," Belinda said. "Mom sent me to live with her for a while."

I chewed on that thought for a bit and then asked, "How come?"

"None of your business," she snapped. "Don't you have papers to deliver?"

I jumped to my feet. Man, this girl was hard to understand.

"Just trying to be friendly," I said as I rode away.

When I passed Mae's house on my way home, Mae was standing on the porch waiting for me. The black and white dog was there, too. Belinda knelt to place a bowl in front of him. His ribs poked out like he hadn't eaten much lately, and his fur was all ruffled. A bit of frayed rope trailed from his neck like someone had tied him up.

"James, come over here," Mae called.

The last time I had left Mae's house, I had been running with rags tied around my head trying to escape Damon's ghost and a swarm of wasps that wanted to eat me alive, so I was more nervous than a twenty-pound gobbler on Thanksgiving as I turned my bike into her driveway.

Now that I knew she was Damon's wife, I felt positively unhinged. What do you say to a woman who has lost her husband when you are the one who found his body, stole his wallet, and then kept his money hidden where a nasty gerbil could chew it up?

I dropped my bike in the driveway and looked everywhere but at Mae.

"James," she said, "I want you to meet my granddaughter."

Well, that was better than saying, "I want to rip your head off for stealing the money I so desperately needed to live on these last few months."

I stepped onto the porch as Belinda straightened. Mae gestured to her with a sweep of her big arm.

"Belinda, this is James. He mows the lawn for me."

"Hey," I said.

Belinda scowled at me.

Mae's head swiveled back and forth between us.

"You know each other?"

I nodded. "We have history class together."

Mae smiled. "Belinda, why didn't you tell me?"

Belinda shrugged.

"Sit down. I'll get the cookies."

WALLS OF GLASS

We sat while Mae bustled into the house.

"What?" I said to Belinda, who kept scowling. She pointed an accusing finger at me. "Don't you dare tell her about the fight," she growled.

I held up my hands in surrender. "I wasn't going to."

Mae came back, and we started in on the cookies.

"Belinda is from Alabama," Mae said. "My daughter sent her to stay with me for a while."

I nodded, but I kept my mouth full so I wouldn't have to say anything.

Mae studied the table for a minute and then looked up as if she had made a decision.

"I guess I should tell you, James, that I found out a few weeks ago that my husband died in a tragic accident."

I gulped down the cookie and choked.

When I could breathe again, I said, "How did he die?"

This question had been torturing me for months.

Mae lifted her shoulders in a despairing way, and I wanted to cry.

"I don't know," she whispered. Her lips quivered. "He was the man they found down in Stillwater Creek. It was all over the news. As a paperboy, you must have seen it."

I nodded, trying to hear over the pounding of my heart. A frog had crawled into my throat, and I blinked at the sting in my eyes.

"I'm sorry," I croaked.

I wanted to tell her I was sorry for everything. That I was sorry my deformed brain had made me do something so stupid as to steal that wallet. I wanted to fall down on my knees and beg her forgiveness. But I could imagine her snatching up my chair and beating me with it if I confessed my crimes. I wouldn't blame her if she did. I wanted to do all of this, but my tongue stuck to the top of my mouth. All I could manage was a nod.

Belinda was glowering at me again. I wanted to distract her attention, so I swallowed, unglued my tongue, and blurted out one of the questions that had been haunting me for months.

"How come he was in the creek?"

Belinda's gaze shifted to Mae, and her pale blue eyes grew wide in interest.

Mae shook her head. Tears blossomed in her eyes, and I felt really stupid again. I never could say the right thing.

"The police think he was robbed because the thief took his wallet only to return it later without the money."

"Money?" I choked.

"Insurance money," Mae said. "Damon had cashed in his life insurance policy because he had been laid off when the factory closed."

A sick knot twisted my stomach. The cookies slithered right back up my throat. I was that thief! I took the money, but I couldn't give it back to her because of that stupid gerbil. If I ever saw that pink-eyed demon again...

I sipped the lemonade, trying to swallow the knot of half-digested cookies that blocked my throat. Mae wiped at a tear that glistened against her dark skin. Then she laid a hand on Belinda's arm.

"But Belinda is here to keep me company now," she said.

The dog hopped up onto the steps and curled up. At least *he* enjoyed a clear conscience.

When I left Mae's house, I wanted to crawl into a hole somewhere and go to sleep like Rip Van Winkle. All this time, Mae had been grieving over her husband, while I worried about being the new kid in town. I had betrayed her trust in me without even meaning to. She thought I was a nice kid—when I was the monster with the deformed brain that had ruined her life.

I couldn't go home—not with the weight of all of my sins pressing on my chest like a semi-truck. I retreated to the park, struggling to keep the tears in. I collapsed onto the bridge and gazed out to where I first met Damon. I could still see Damon's body slouching against that log all pitiful and diminished as the turtles and birds pecked away at him. Mae had loved him. She had needed him. And I only thought of myself. Tears dripped from my eyes. How could I keep all that shame and sadness bottled up inside me?

Something wet touched my hand, and I jerked to find the dog

with his tongue hanging out one side of his mouth.

"What do you want?" I snapped. He blinked at me and raised his floppy ears. Then he nuzzled my hand, and I raised it to pat his head. He wagged his tail, and I hugged his neck as I wept. I wished I had never come to Oklahoma or to this stupid park. I wished I had never found Damon or his money.

"Why didn't you tell me?" I whispered to Damon's ghost. "I could have given it to her months ago."

The dog sat on his haunches while I sobbed into his matted fur. He seemed to know what I needed. I opened my mouth to say something else when someone thumped me on the back of the head. I released the dog and jerked around to see my big brother glaring down at me.

"Where've you been? Mom's looking for you."

He saw me wipe at the tears.

"What are you blubbering about? School?" His gaze ran over me from head to toe. "You don't look like you got into a fight."

I shook my head.

"If some kid is picking on you, you've got to fight him," he said. "I already told you that."

"Nobody's picking on me," I said as I clambered to my feet.

He glowered at me like he didn't believe me.

"Whose dog is that?" he asked.

"I don't know. He follows me around sometimes."

"Mom's waiting," Clint said, and we walked home. The dog stood on the bridge, wagging his tail as we left.

I guess the guilt and sadness still shone on my face because when Mom saw me, she pulled me into a tight hug. She wore her nursing uniform since she had to go to work, and she smelled like antiseptic.

"Somebody's picking on him at school," Clint said.

Mom held me at arm's length and studied my face. "I'll call the school," she said.

"You can't do that, Mom," Clint replied. "I already told you that. You have to let him fight it out, or it'll only get worse."

Mom's face fell into a tortured frown.

Clint appraised her like he was trying to decide something. "Look, Mom," he said. "This isn't some farm town in Idaho. We're in a city now. At school, we're the minority. There are more blacks in the high school than there are whites. It's probably the same at the junior high. The other high school where the rich kids go is mostly white. James has to learn how to deal with this stuff on his own."

He glanced down at me with a half-pitying, half-disgusted expression.

"If a bunch of kids gets in trouble because you call the principal, they'll really go after him. It would only make it worse."

By this time, the tears were sliding down my mother's cheeks. She stared at the floor. At that moment, I wanted to hug her and tell her all the stupid things I had done since we moved here, just to get it off my chest. But the tortured sorrow on her face and the huge lump that filled my throat meant all I could do was hug her and hope she would still love me after she found out what I had done.

Mom must have forgotten why she wanted me. She left for work without saying anything. I escaped to the safety of my room to work on my reflection drawing because I didn't want to think about the mountain of problems hovering over my head.

Now that Mrs. Took helped me get the picture laid out, I was able to work on it on my own. I focused on the back of my head because every time I tried to work on my face, I got it wrong. Faces were hard to do. It looked like my face more or less, but it was wrong. It should be different somehow.

I erased it and left it blank. That's when I thought of putting my hand on the mirror. I went to the bathroom and stood in front of the big mirror Dawn used to apply her makeup. I reached out and placed my left hand on the mirror. Mrs. Took taught us to draw our own hands already, so I knew how to do it. I studied the image for a while, and, after a few trips back to the bathroom, I was starting to get it. As I was finishing the back of the hand, I smudged too aggressively, and the fingers turned black. I erased the mistake, but the contrast between white and black gave me an idea. I understood what was missing—Belinda. And it wasn't a mirror, it was a wall of glass. Belinda was on the other side looking at me.

CHAPTER TWENTY
FROZEN FRIENDS

hat's your mom like?" I asked Belinda as we sat by the creek in the shade of the birch trees watching the water skippers skim across the surface. They glided together as if they were painting complex geographic designs only they could see.

Belinda wrinkled her nose. "She's like Grandma, only she's a lot thinner."

She glanced at me, trying not to smile, but it twitched at the side of her lips.

"Your grandma is the toughest woman I know," I said. "She attacked a poisonous snake with nothing but a shovel, and she rescued me from a pack of deadly wasps."

Now Belinda cast me a disdainful glance. "They weren't deadly. They were just wasps."

"You weren't the one being stung," I said.

Since this conversation wasn't going my way, I changed subjects. "What's your dad like?"

Now she frowned. "He works a lot. And why are you asking me all these questions?"

"Just curious."

"Look. If we're going to be friends, you have to stop quizzing me every time you see me."

Friends? Did she say friends? I looked away so she wouldn't see me trying to swallow the knot that rose in my throat or blink the tears from my eyes. No one had considered me a friend for so long, I wasn't sure what to say. I wasn't sure I still knew how to be one.

"What do you want me to do then?" I asked.

"Teach me how to play baseball," she said.

Well, that's not what I expected. "Baseball? Why?"

"You're quizzing me again."

"Sorry."

Good grief, how were you supposed to get to know someone if you couldn't ask questions?

Belinda narrowed her eyes. "Because," she said. "I'm sick and tired of looking stupid in gym class, and you seem to know how to play."

"Okay," I said. "But you have to teach me how to fight."

Belinda stared at me in shock for a moment and then flashed a big, toothy grin that was white as cream against her dark skin.

"*That* I know how to do," Belinda said.

It's true that I had a big brother who could teach me how to fight. He did, sort of. Usually when we fought, I lost. Except for the short fight when I tossed the kid over my head, I had only been in one other real fight—and I lost that one, too. In fact, that kid could have messed me up if he'd wanted to. But he was my friend, so he took pity on me and only gave me a shiner.

The days slid into weeks as I settled into the routine of two paper routes, school, working on my drawings, going to church, playing baseball, and trading punches with Belinda. We didn't really hit each other—well except for the time I accidentally bloodied her nose.

Thanksgiving and Christmas came and went as the weather turned foul, until one morning in mid-January I awoke to find a layer of white covering the world as if God had become tired of the drab, leafless trees and decided to decorate them with a sheet of glistening ice.

The trees sagged under the weight of their frozen blanket. My street looked like a war zone. Branches snapped off. Trees sagged on each other as if seeking support in bearing the weight of the clumps of snow and ice that clung to them. Long, thick icicles stabbed toward the earth at weird angles. All of this surprised me because it had only been raining when I had fallen into bed the night before.

Clint, who had also picked up a morning paper route, woke me up at 4:30 a.m. to tell me we didn't have to deliver papers that morning. I was too groggy to care why, so I just jerked the covers back over my head and kept snoring. By the time I made my way to the front room a few hours later, Clint was already up and shrugging on his coat. I hurried after him.

"No school today," he said as he yanked on his gloves.

"It only snowed a few inches," I said in surprise.

In Idaho, they didn't cancel school until there were a few feet of drifting snow. Newspapers never canceled their delivery. But when I got outside, it took me all of five seconds to figure out why.

I dragged my bike off the porch and rode it across the lawn, listening to the frozen grass crackle and pop under my tires. I hopped off the curb onto the unplowed road, and, before I knew it, I was soaring like a cardinal as my bike popped out from underneath me. I slammed onto the frozen ground and kept sliding across the street in slow spirals as my bike zipped off in the opposite direction. The thick layer of ice underneath the snow made it impossible for anyone to drive a car or ride a bike. Stillwater simply closed down. Not even the stores opened.

My somersault onto the road so shocked me that I lay in the middle of the street staring up at the wisps of white clouds in the aqua-blue sky until an ice-cold snowball slammed into my face. I scrambled up to wage war with Clint. Then we set to building an igloo. It was a slushy, sagging thing with more holes in it than Swiss cheese. We tried to keep the holes patched up, but bits of the walls and ceilings flopped out.

When we sloshed back inside, soaked to the skin and cold as Popsicles, I found the pink-eyed gerbil standing on top of the dresser. She froze for an instant with that deer-in-the-headlights look. She had returned to the scene of the crime, but she didn't look too good. Her tail hadn't grown back. The stiff bone stuck out white and sharp like a long toothpick. Her fur was shabby. Her eye twitched more than usual. She rubbed her front paws together, and I knew she had come searching for food or maybe a nice cozy nest of one hundred-dollar bills.

"Stupid rat," I said. "Freedom isn't as easy as having someone feed you all the time, is it?"

She wiggled her whiskers and flew off the table. I launched my boot at her, but it flew past her, and she disappeared under the bed again.

The papers had to go out the next day even though every other business was still closed. I nearly killed myself trying to cross the streets in the pitch-black morning. But the ice sure made it a lot faster getting down the hills.

I helped Mae and Belinda shovel. Afterward we engaged in a wild snowball fight. Belinda's aim was getting a lot better, but I still won. All while we played, I tried to figure out how to tell them what I had done. I would have enough money by the end of the month to make up for the bills the pink-eyed gerbil chewed up. But how do you tell someone something like that? I was only in seventh grade, and this was a problem for a fully-formed brain— not a pea-sized boy brain.

When I got home, Mom and Dad sat on two kitchen chairs in front of Dawn and Clint, who perched on the couch. Their long faces and darting eyes told me something was wrong. My heart crawled up into my throat, making it hard to breathe. I glanced around for the police officer, but no one else was there.

"Sit down," Dad said. He waved a tired hand toward the couch.

I sat and tried to swallow.

Dad wrung his hands. Mom dabbed at a tear.

"We need to ask for your help," Dad said. "The car needs a new timing belt and water pump. It's going to cost a lot of money. We can't pay for the repair *and* keep food on the table."

He glanced at Mom. She blinked. Mom's eyes were red-rimmed. Her face was pale. Dad kept squeezing his hands together. They both looked wretched—like this was difficult for them.

"We hate to ask you," Dad said, "but it would be a real help if you all could lend us some money to help pay for the repair."

All of a sudden, I could breathe again. Was that all? I almost jumped up and handed them every cent I owned—I was so relieved that I wasn't the problem. Then I remembered what I needed that money for and the bottom of my stomach disappeared with a swooping sickness. If I gave them the money, I wouldn't be able to tell Mae what I had done for at least another month, maybe two.

Dad's nervous wringing of his hands, and Mom's quiet shame convinced me. I couldn't abandon my family.

"How much do you need?" Clint said.

"The repair will cost eight hundred dollars."

There was nothing else to do but give them a share from my paper route money. I tried to look on the bright side. This meant I had more time to figure out how to tell Mae what I had done.

CHAPTER TWENTY-ONE
THE DARKNESS OF MY PEOPLE

As Mrs. Took examined my reflection drawing, her eyebrows kept bouncing up and down. I finished the picture of myself looking through the wall of glass. I drew myself with my back facing the viewer. The back of the head was mine, thin with big ears and straight hair. But Belinda looked back at me through the wall of glass. I tried to capture the expression on her face like the one I made when I was thinking of Damon—kind of sad and frightened. We each placed a hand on the glass wall between us. My arm and hand were pale white, while hers were a rich dark black. It was just light and shadows, white and black. They weren't opposites. They were a pair. They belonged together, like me and Damon.

When Mrs. Took glanced up at me, she was frowning. "How did you come up with this idea?" she asked.

"Uh, I made a mistake, and I liked it."

"I'm not sure I can display this in the classroom," she said.

I studied the picture again, trying to see what I had done wrong.

She pinched her lips into a thin line. When I didn't say anything, she continued. "You've made a racial statement here that might upset a lot of people."

Panic rose in my chest. "I have?"

She nodded. "This is the magic of art, James. Without even realizing it, you've captured the conflicted hypocrisy of our society."

WALLS OF GLASS

I glanced down at my picture. I didn't have any idea what she was talking about.

"You still don't see it, do you?"

"Um." I swallowed.

She frowned, rubbed a finger over her lips, then passed a hand across the back of her neck.

"You know what you are?" she asked.

I watched her because I knew she didn't expect an answer.

"You're a budding humanist."

My gaze strayed to the bright paintings awash in color that stood all over the room and then back to my drawing. I knew I was human, and I had drawn some humans, but I had no idea what a humanist was.

Mrs. Took laughed out loud as she looked at me. "'Don't act like I'm speaking a different language," she said and then pointed at my picture. "You see all humans as basically good with the same fundamental needs, and you are able to capture some of the deepest human emotions, like sadness, love, fear, and even the need to belong."

"I do?" I asked bending closer to look at my picture. How could she tell all of that from a black and white pencil drawing?

Mrs. Took pursed her lips in thought and tapped my picture with her finger. "You see the world in full color," she said. "And you don't appear to judge people by the color of their skin. By some miracle, you've managed to escape the hypocrisy of our society, which is, perhaps, why you can draw it."

I stared at her, not sure I understood what she meant.

She smiled and shook her head at my ignorance. "Innocent as babes," she mumbled. "Look," she pointed to the picture again. "You portray the white boy and the black girl as equals separated by an invisible wall that keeps them artificially apart. Their attempt to be friends is rupturing the social barriers our society seeks to reinforce and perpetuate."

Then she pursed her lips together and made a decision.

"Can I borrow this?" she asked.

"I guess."

"And do I have your permission to talk to your parents about this?"

WALLS OF GLASS

"Uh, what for?" The picture wasn't perfect, but I liked it. I couldn't see why she would need to talk to my parents unless I had done something wrong. I glanced at the drawing again, trying to figure out where I messed up.

Now she grinned. "You're not in trouble," she said. "I just want to ask their permission—and yours—to enter this in an art contest the university art department is sponsoring next month."

"I don't want people to laugh at me," I said. I hadn't been drawing long, and I knew I still had a lot to learn. Besides, I already had more problems than my little brain could handle.

She placed a hand on my arm. "Oh, they won't laugh," she said.

The new sex education segment we began in science class the next day drove my drawing from my mind. I don't know what anybody else thought about the class because I was too embarrassed to talk about it. If I could have crawled off into some dark corner and disappeared, I would have. I hadn't thought much about sex, but when I was little, I convinced myself babies just came out of the mother's stomach through a slit that magically opened in her side. It made sense at the time.

I never thought to ask how the babies got there. The more Mr. Ward talked about procreation, the more I knew I didn't want to know. Then they split us into two groups, boys in one room and girls in another. They showed the boys a cartoon film about boy development while they showed the girls a cartoon about girls. Then they made us switch movies. After that, they ushered us into the same room and asked if anyone had any questions.

After a few crude comments from the boys in the back and some nervous giggles from the girls, a deathly silence settled over us. I'm not sure what they expected us to do. But I've never met the kid who wanted to talk about his own body in front of a bunch of strangers.

Why is it that adults have complete amnesia when it comes to remembering what it was like to be a kid? I hadn't understood much, but I wasn't going to ask. The one thing I did notice was that all the kids in the cartoons were white. I glanced around at the room filled mostly with black kids, but they didn't seem to notice. Or maybe they were used to the fact that none of the kids in the videos they showed us ever looked like them.

At lunch, I fled to Mrs. Took's room to work on my new drawing. The black girl and white kid fought again in between classes. The image of him raising his hands to protect his head with an expression of fear on his face as the black girl brought her book down on his head stuck with me.

That moment froze in my memory and begged to be drawn. I always thought the kid liked fighting, but now I knew he fought because he had no choice. This made me wonder about the black girl. Why did she fight all the time? Why did she go after Belinda? What were the secret terrors that haunted her at night?

This time, I drew a picture of a white boy kneeling on the asphalt peering up between his arms. I sketched in curly black hair. One arm he raised was white. The other was black.

Belinda sat studiously working on something else while I drew. Mrs. Took came over to check on my drawing. After a few suggestions, she turned to Belinda.

"What are you working on?" she asked.

Belinda glanced up and then back down. She moved her pen aside so Mrs. Took could see the words.

"Just a poem," she said.

"Ah," Mrs. Took said, "you're an artist, too, then."

Belinda shrugged.

"May I?" Mrs. Took held out a hand.

Belinda handed her the paper. Mrs. Took's eyes shifted back and forth, and she nodded. "You *are* an artist." Then her gaze bobbled between us. "Do you two realize you're writing and drawing about the same questions?"

I raised my eyebrows at Belinda. Was I drawing about a question?

"Listen to this, James." Mrs. Took read the poem out loud.

WALLS OF GLASS

J.W. ELLIOT

"'Imprisoned in the Darkness of my People
By Belinda Washington

How black is black?
When are you black enough, but not too black?
Why should I explain the coal dust painted on my skin?
If God is the artist whose brush strokes shaped me,
Why should I be ashamed of who I am?

Some white folks say they see no color.
Others wish they didn't see me at all.
Some black folks say I'm way too black,
Does my color mean I have to crawl?

If you would look beneath the skin,
You might find a person, strong or feeble.
Instead, the walls you build close me in.
I am imprisoned in the darkness of my people.'"

Mrs. Took finished reading, and her face fell into a frown.
"It must be hard for kids your age, trapped between the inno-
cence of childhood and the grim reality of adulthood."
She sat down, letting the paper fall into her lap with a jingle of
bracelets and shook her head. Her eyes filled with tears.
"What kind of world are we leaving for you?" she murmured.

CHAPTER TWENTY-TWO
ZERO AND OREO

Who was the clown that thought it was a good idea to have kids fill out Valentine's Day cards for each other? I don't know, but I was sure grateful we didn't have to do that anymore in seventh grade. I didn't mind the chocolate. But the silly, insincere notes and outright lies sprinkled with nasty comments and insults ruined the entire holiday. I already knew I was a piece of work. I didn't need anyone else telling me. Still, I helped my little brothers do theirs for their school classes. They were all excited, but I worried someone might be mean to them the way they had been to me.

I skipped the holiday. Romance was for momma's boys and movies. But I did enjoy a few *Zero* candy bars and some *Reese's Peanut Butter Cups* because, well, it's a sin not to have sugar and chocolate on Valentine's Day.

Mrs. Took must have thought I needed a valentine because she was standing at the front door of the school waiting for me—which creeped me out. Teachers aren't supposed to do that, especially on Valentine's Day. She was smiling and holding out a newspaper.

"Did your parents tell you?" she asked.

"Tell me what?"

"You took second place in the contest!"

"What contest?"

She pointed to a photograph of my wall of glass drawing printed in the newspaper. I didn't read the newspapers. I just delivered them. If it wasn't on the front page, I never saw it.

"They announced it yesterday," she said. "I thought your father would have seen it."

My father was working and going to school. He didn't have time to read the newspaper.

"You've won fifty dollars," she said. "You have to go to the awards ceremony to pick it up."

When I didn't say anything, she said, "I'll call your parents and explain. This is a real honor, James. You should be very proud. No junior high school student has placed in the contest in ten years."

Well, I *was* proud until I found a copy of my drawing taped to my locker with a burning cross drawn over it in red ink. I tore it down and yanked open my locker to find a piece of paper sitting on top of my books. "Traitor," it read.

Mrs. Took was right. They weren't going to laugh. My life became very unpleasant. It's not like anyone had talked to me much before, but now even their glances were hostile. I tried to go to the swing at recess because I didn't feel like drawing after all this, but somehow the tennis balls always seemed to fly in my direction. After one hit me in the head, I gave up and escaped inside.

I met Belinda coming out of the cafeteria, so we plopped down on the stairs to talk. I pulled out my last two *Zero* bars and offered her one.

She wrinkled her nose. "Thanks, but I don't like them."

"What's not to like?" I asked as I peeled back the silver-blue wrapper and sank my teeth into the creamy white fudge that covered the dark nougat. As I swallowed, a tennis ball bounced past us. I glanced up to see Leroy and Oscar striding toward us. The fact that the two of them were together was enough to make me sweat.

Oscar's gaze flicked to my candy bar.

"Look. It's the Zero Boy," he said.

Leroy laughed. "You're a zero at everything," he said. "You and your little Oreo girlfriend."

"Leave us alone," Belinda said.

She stood, so I did, too. I couldn't let her seem tougher than me.

WALLS OF GLASS

"Zero and Oreo," Oscar chanted. "You're a match. He's black on the inside and white on the outside, and you're white on the inside and black on the outside."

"Shut up," Belinda said.

Now other kids took up the chant. "Zero and Oreo. Zero and Oreo."

I glanced at Belinda, hoping she would let it drop so we could get the heck out of there. But she didn't look scared. Even with Belinda's coaching, I wasn't prepared for a real fight.

I reached over and grabbed her arm. She shook me loose and punched Leroy right in the nose. Oscar jumped in and pulled me into a headlock. His big fist found my face, and he proceeded to leave his knuckle prints all over the place. I figured this was one of those times when I had to fight back. If I didn't, Clint would disown me.

There was no way to avoid the fight now, so I did what I had been taught to do in Judo. I punched him in the groin with one hand, reached over his head with the other, and dug my fingers into his eyes. As his head came back, I drove my knee into the back of his leg.

He fell back onto the stairs, but he came up spitting mad. Judo got me out of the headlock, but now I had bigger problems. I blinked at the stinging sweat in my eyes and swallowed the blood in my mouth.

As Oscar drew back his fist, I lost it. I completely lost my sanity. I screamed or growled or something and rushed him. I plowed into him with my head down and my fists flying like I was crazy. I guess I was crazy—crazy scared.

We careened onto the stairs. He grunted and let go of me as the stairs took him in the ribs. I scrambled to my feet and spun to see what had happened to Belinda. I found her on Leroy's back with her legs wrapped around his waist and her arms around his throat. She gave a scream like some warrior princess that echoed off the walls. What had I been worried about? She knew what she was doing.

Oscar's fist slammed into my head, and I fell sideways onto the stairs as he bellowed something. The crowd parted like the Red Sea when Moses raised his staff, and three or four teachers

113

dragged us apart.

I crawled to my feet and stood there, blinking and trembling and trying not to cry. I wiped at the sweat on my face with the back of my hand and stared at the blood. Belinda stood proud and silent while Leroy gasped for breath. Oscar didn't look at me, but his friends did. I was in serious trouble.

The principal made me call Dad to pick me up because he kicked us out of school for the day. On the way home, Dad asked, "Did you start it?"

"No."

"Did you finish it?"

Well, we hadn't gotten around to finishing the fight because the teachers broke it up, but I did get hit last.

"I guess so," I lied.

"Good. I've told you before I don't want you starting any fights, but you have a right to defend yourself."

Dad might not give me any grief, but if Clint found out a girl had been teaching me how to fight, I didn't know what he might do—stuff me in a pillowcase and toss me in the creek like people did to cats they didn't want. But my lie worked because Clint patted me on the back with a big smile when he heard Dad tell Mom what happened.

"See, I told you," he beamed. "That kid won't pick on you again."

I wasn't so sure about that.

CHAPTER TWENTY-THREE
WHITE OR BLACK,
IT'S ALL THE SAME

That evening, when I saw the round, puffy afro bobbing above the cars parked on the other side of Main Street, I hit the brakes and pulled my bike up behind a big, brown trash can. I had never seen Leroy down here. I knew for a fact he lived over by Boomer Creek. He was pushing some big black man in a wheelchair. My bruises were healing, but they still hurt enough to remind me what Leroy and Oscar had done to Belinda and me.

I thought I understood Oscar. With a dad like his, I was surprised Oscar wasn't in jail already. But I didn't know much about Leroy. He wasn't in any of my classes. I couldn't figure out why he hated Belinda. She was black like him, and black kids stuck together. This didn't fit with what Mae had been trying to tell me about discrimination either. In a case like this, I did the only natural thing. I followed him.

My bike, with my newspaper bag swinging from the handlebars, made me obvious, so I hopped off and walked the bike as I struggled to stay out of sight. The breeze blew cold, which gave me an excuse to pull up the hood on my sweatshirt. Leroy was easy to follow because his big, bushy afro stood out against the redbrick buildings of downtown Stillwater.

I wondered if Leroy planned to dump the crippled man in some alleyway and rob him. Seemed like the kind of thing Leroy would do.

They passed the drugstore and the hardware store while I kept a good distance, trying to look like I was window shopping. I stayed alert in case I had to ride for help when Leroy made his move. But Leroy passed all the dark alleys. They paused when the black and white lop-eared dog padded up to them. He raised up and put his paws on the guy in the wheelchair and panted with his tail wagging as they patted him.

"Traitor," I breathed. I had convinced myself the dog had a special liking for me, only to see it wasn't me he liked at all. He liked everybody, even the kid that had been chucking tennis balls at my head for the past few months. The dog bounded away to nuzzle somebody else's hand, and they kept going until they turned toward a small, white Baptist church.

I read the sign twice to make sure, my eyes weren't deceiving me. Leroy didn't seem like the church-going kind. I ditched my bike half a block away, while Leroy pushed the wheelchair up a long, sloping ramp. I crept around to peek in a side window.

Leroy sat on a bench beside the man in the wheelchair, who seemed to be holding a photo. Leroy bowed his head. I could see now that the guy in the wheelchair didn't have any legs. His stumps bulged beneath the flaps of his jeans that had been folded and pinned back. He was a large, black man with a shaved head, and he wore a white T-shirt.

I sneaked around to the front door and slipped inside before crouching behind a solid, wooden banister to peek around the corner. Their voices echoed off the white plastered walls. Rows of benches sat silent and brooding all around them. The man was shaking his head as he stared down at the picture in his hands.

"Don't ever let 'em make you feel like you're less than a man," he said. His voice was deep with a thick southern accent that echoed in the empty hall.

Leroy's afro bobbed.

"The Viet Cong over in Vietnam had it right," the man continued. "They dropped pamphlets that said, 'They call us gooks here, and they call you cotton pickers over there. You're the same as us. Get out, it's not your fight.'"

"That kind of stuff got to a lot of the guys 'cause we knew it was true. Here we were fighting for our country when our country didn't even want us. Our officers treated us like dogs. I think the gooks knew it."

The man laid the picture in his lap and wheeled himself to the front of the church until he was staring up at the giant, wooden cross that hung there.

"One day," he continued, "we got ambushed from three sides. The gooks let us walk right into it before they opened up. After they shot us up a bit, they just stopped shooting. Then one of them gooks called out in perfect English. 'Go home, soul man. This ain't your war.' Then they melted into the jungle."

The man shook his head.

"I was in one patrol where they let our point man, who was a black dude, walk right past them, and then they shot the white guy behind him. They let all the soul brothers walk past and only shot at the white boys."

He turned his wheelchair around to gaze at Leroy. I could see the scars that ran up the side of his face and crawled to the top of his bald head.

"That kind of stuff gets you thinking," he said. "We knew they were trying to stir up racial tension. But we had been dragged over there to kill those people, and what had they done to us? When I got back to the barracks, I got treated like I wasn't a US citizen. I got treated worse than the Viet Cong. The officers wouldn't let us have any soul music, they wouldn't promote us, and when they did, the white chuckies refused to follow the orders of a black man. Some boys got so angry they rolled flash grenades into the officer's tents to give 'em a scare. Some of those officers died, and I started wondering if I should go home."

He rolled up to Leroy again and lifted the picture to stare at it.

"I did things," he said. "I saw things that no human being should ever do or see." His voice became so soft I had to lean in to hear him.

When he didn't continue right away, I considered leaving. I felt dirty listening to a private conversation like this. But the man continued, and I was so enthralled by his story I couldn't leave.

"Once I saw my buddy go down," he said, "so I grabbed him up and tried to drag him away, but his leg came off. I picked up his leg, stuck his boot in my pocket, and dragged him off the battlefield. When I looked down at him, all he said was this: 'Dwight, this ain't our war. This ain't our war.'

"After that, I told 'em I wasn't gonna fight no more. They would have to send me home. I wasn't gonna kill for 'em anymore. And I sure wasn't going to die for 'em. So they put me in a prison, a marine prison. They said the only way I was going home was with a dishonorable discharge or in a body bag even though I had spent a full year fighting and killing for 'em and watching my friends die around me. I even had a purple heart.

"Then we got word they had shot The King. They killed Martin Luther King. That was the last straw. We rose up. We attacked 'em. They had to learn they couldn't treat us that way. That our blood was just as good as their blood. That our blood had been spilt just like theirs. But it didn't do no good. They sent in marines, a bunch of white marines and a few black ones, and they put us down."

Leroy spoke for the first time.

"Uncle Dwight," he said. "What happened to your legs?"

I knew I should leave, but the question glued me to the spot with that same morbid fascination that had drawn me back to Damon's corpse. I leaned in closer to the cool wall, not wanting to miss a single word.

Dwight never lifted his gaze from the photograph.

"They took me out and put me on the line again," Dwight continued as if Leroy hadn't spoken. "I told 'em one more mission, and I was going home. We were coming across a rice paddy when the gooks opened up on us with mortar rounds and heavy machine guns. This new white boy that none of the brothers liked 'cuz he kept harassing us took a few rounds in the chest. We opened up, but the Viet Cong took off running. Our lieutenant ordered us to chase 'em down and kill 'em. But he told me to take the white boy back to the medivac choppers.

"The boy was staring up at me with big, wide eyes. I wanted to leave him 'cuz I knew he wasn't gonna live, but I picked him up and carried him back to the edge of the paddy. When the firing erupted again, I turned to see all our boys being mowed down. Them gooks had drawn 'em into an ambush.

WALLS OF GLASS

"I scrambled out of the paddy and stepped on a mine that blew both my legs off. I remember watching my boot with my foot still in it flying through the air to land up in a banana tree. It slid down the leaves and splashed into the water of the rice paddy. And that was it. They had to send me home then. Crippled. Useless."

My stomach churned. Leroy bowed his head to stare at Dwight's two stumps.

"And the white boy?" Leroy asked.

Now Dwight raised his head. "He was dead before I got to the edge of the paddy."

Quiet filled the church as the world became a much more complicated place for me. How was anyone supposed to know who to trust when everyone seemed to have these secret, selfish motives? Why did people treat each other with such hatred? Before I could decide anything, Dwight started speaking again.

"I don't want to make it sound like 'Nam was a picnic for the white boys," he said. "It wasn't. We all suffered. We still suffer."

Dwight laid a hand on his thigh.

"When we got back, they didn't give us brothers anything. I met a South Vietnamese man I knew over in 'Nam, and he was running a business and driving a nice car. Uppity black boys who went to college instead of going to war called us baby killers and pranced around in their business suits. What have I got for serving my country? Nothin'."

Dwight's face tightened in anger. "I'm telling you, Leroy, you be careful who you trust. You gotta fight for your rights, boy. And no matter what happens to you, you don't ever let 'em make you feel like you're less than a man." Dwight's hand strayed to one of his stump legs again. "White or black, it's all the same."

I didn't want to hear anymore. I backed out of the chapel as quiet as I could, picked up my bike, and rode home. If what Dwight said was true, then I could understand why the black kids didn't want to play with the white kids. But Dwight seemed to be talking about white people and Vietnamese people the same way they talked about him. He acted like they were all the same. But I wasn't like Oscar. Belinda wasn't like Leroy. They were just people, weren't they?

CHAPTER TWENTY-FOUR
NEWS FROM MOBILE

I survived February without another fight or a spanking, mostly because I hid out in Mrs. Took's room with Belinda. *Zero* wrappers kept finding their way into my locker. One day, my whole locker was covered with them, and they had been glued on. My homeroom teacher made me clean them off with a razor blade and water—like it was my fault.

Spring break came in mid-March with a vicious series of rainstorms that kept us inside most of the week. I wondered what the storm waters would wash into the canal this time. After hearing Dwight's story, I was afraid to scramble around too much on the bank. I knew I was being stupid, but anybody could have left a booby trap for me to step on. And I didn't think I could stand finding another corpse or some mangled body part. When I went to check the creek, I made sure I stayed on the bridge, but all I found was the usual leftovers of other people's lives, tossed out, lost and forlorn because no one wanted them anymore.

Belinda and Mae drove off to Alabama to visit Belinda's family, and, since I didn't have any other friends, I hung around the house annoying Mom with mice until she threatened to beat me to within an inch of my life.

I retreated to the kitchen table to finish my drawing of the kid with the raised hands. After that, I got bored. I set traps for the pink-eyed devil. She'd been chewing through my socks and made another nest in my drawer.

The next morning the news broke. It wasn't front page, but Clint found it. Then it appeared on the evening news. "Nineteen-Year-Old Black Man Murdered in Mobile, Alabama."

Belinda was from Mobile, so I paid close attention. Some white guy in a suit said, "Look, I think it's sad, but where was all the media attention when a black man murdered a white police officer in cold blood? Black men sat on that jury, and they couldn't even reach a decision."

At first, they reported that the black man, named Michael Donald, had been selling drugs. But his mom didn't believe them. She called in Jesse Jackson and the civil rights people to protest. The whole story turned my stomach into a boiling cauldron of snakes, and I paced around the room while the news broadcaster spoke. What if Damon had been murdered like Michael, and all I did about it was steal his wallet?

Mae and Belinda were in Mobile while all this was going on. For all I knew, they might be related to Michael. When Belinda didn't come to school on Monday morning, I stopped by Mae's house to see if they were home. The little, white house stood silent as death, which made me even more nervous. I peddled past Mae's house three or four times a day, wishing I knew their address in Alabama so I could write to see if they were okay.

That night, I almost catapulted off the sofa when I saw Mae and Belinda on the news. Mae had on a billowing, white blouse. Belinda wore a frilly, pink dress. They were standing around the tree where the young man had been hanged. The light of the candles they held glimmered in the darkness and shone off of their dark skin. Seeing Belinda standing next to a bunch of other black people made me realize how black she was. I wondered if Mae, who was now an old woman and a grade school teacher, was going to become an activist again.

When I saw Mae's white car parked in her driveway on Wednesday, I didn't even hesitate. I peddled my bike right up to her porch, leapt up the steps, and banged on the door. Mae opened it. She nodded and gestured for me to come in. The house still smelled of mothballs, but the aroma of frying chicken laced the air.

"I saw you on the news," I blurted.

Not very tactful, but after days of suspense, I couldn't keep it in. They were at the vigil. They must have had all the juicy news.

Mae nodded again. "I wish I could do more for that poor woman," she said.

Belinda stepped out of the kitchen with a rag in her hands.

"Hey," I said.

I wanted to ask what it had been like, but she didn't give me a welcoming smile.

"Oh," I said glancing at Mae. "I'm sorry."

My face burned with shame. The way I barged in on them you would think they were the only friends I had in the world. I guess they were, but I don't think they knew that.

I turned to leave, but Mae placed a hand on my arm.

"James," she said, "I would have stayed in Mobile for the protests if I was younger and didn't have a job to look after."

Belinda tossed the towel over her shoulder and came to stand beside Mae.

"I was jailed nine times before I was twenty," Mae said. "I was beaten up twice, once by the police, because I dared to speak out. Things are better now in some places. But—"

She shook her head and pursed her lips. "Black men are still getting killed because of the color of their skin."

"They said it was drugs," I said.

Mae's eyes blazed. "Drugs didn't have anything to do with it," she snapped. "That boy was walking home from the store."

"Sorry," I said again. "I didn't mean you were wrong. I was only saying what they reported on the news." But that wasn't entirely true. I had never stopped to consider that, as black people, they might have experienced the lynching very differently than I had. To me it was a horrible curiosity and a reason to be concerned about them. But to Mae it was deeply personal in a way I didn't think I could ever understand.

Mae's expression softened. "Please understand, James. This has been a very difficult time for me because—" she paused, and I knew she was thinking about Damon.

I glanced at his picture. He looked down on me with a grandfatherly smile. His face was the kind that made you feel like you had to like him—as if he liked you even though he hadn't met you. A nervous shiver ran through me. Had somebody killed Damon and dumped his body in the creek? I bit my lip. This secret had been eating me up inside for months. I couldn't keep it in any longer. Mae deserved to know, especially after what she had been through.

The smell of mothballs seemed to grow stronger as the blood pounded in my ears. I steeled myself as I turned back to tell Mae that I had found Damon in the creek, but she was already speaking.

"We just need to be left alone for a spell," she said. "We knew Michael Donald. He was a good boy."

The admission of guilt froze on my tongue, and my courage failed me. I couldn't say it.

"Okay," I said with a little shrug. I raised a hand to Belinda. "I'll see you at school."

Belinda gave me a sad smile as if she suspected what had been going through my mind.

CHAPTER TWENTY-FIVE
THE DARKNESS WITHIN

Thursday night, I drove with my parents to the awards ceremony for my drawing of the glass wall. It's hard not to grin and get butterflies fluttering around in your belly when people you don't even know tell you how much your drawing meant to them. And it's hard not to get that creepy, wriggly sensation in your chest when adults look at you sideways as if they're contemplating doing something terrible to you. My picture also embarrassed me because I saw a lot of artwork that made my drawing look simple and uninspired.

Still, I left the ceremony with a fifty dollar check in my pocket and a warm feeling in my chest which lasted only until some drunk guy stumbled up to me. Dad stiff-armed the man to keep him back, and we tried to keep walking. But the drunk reached around my dad, grabbed my wrist, and yanked me around. I found myself staring into the watery, blood-shot eyes of the man that kicked Oscar out of the convenience store. I tried to jerk free, but he was a lot stronger than I was.

"You're that coon lover my boy's been telling me about," he growled.

His sour breath washed over my face. If I could have jumped into hyperspace right then, I would have been in the next county in less than a second. My knees went weak. My stomach did a somersault. His lip curled up, and he opened his mouth to say something, but Dad knocked his hand away and shoved him back. Dad grabbed me by the arm and marched me towards the car. As we reached it, something slammed into my back. I cried out in surprise, thinking the drunk had attacked me. Then I felt something wet through my shirt. Dad shoved me into the car and stood over Mom while she clambered in. Then he roared away in the puke mobile like he was flying an X-wing fighter. Another egg hit the back window before we careened out of the parking lot.

Mom peered back at me. Tears glistened on her cheeks. "Are you okay?" she asked.

I blinked and nodded, trying to swallow the fear that seized my throat like a noose. I remembered what Mrs. Took had said. They didn't laugh at me. They hated me. Was fifty bucks worth it?

That night, I crouched in the shadows of the hallway afraid to go to bed and determined to hear what my parents would say when they thought I wasn't listening.

"I knew we shouldn't have taken him," I heard my dad say.

"But it was an honor, and it's a really good drawing," Mom replied.

"I understand that," Dad said. "But I know for a fact that two of the judges voted against it because they said it would only stir up racial tension. One of my professors asked me about it today. He did *not* look pleased."

"It was just a picture of a boy and girl," Mom protested. "Anyway, he's just a child."

My dad cut in. "He's a child who sees more than adults are willing to admit."

They were quiet for a long time.

"I don't know," Dad said. "Maybe it isn't worth it."

After surveying the floor of my bedroom to make sure the little gerbil monster wasn't waiting to sink her needle-sharp teeth into my big toe, I crawled into bed to stare at the shifting shadows on the ceiling. Was it worth it? Did Dad mean me? Or did he mean living in Oklahoma? Why would people hate me for a simple drawing? It wasn't just kids now. It was adults.

Maybe Belinda could explain it. She knew more about it than I did.

When I asked her the next day, she smirked at me like I was as dim as a burned out light bulb.

"Don't you pay attention to anything?" she demanded.

I scowled. "It's just a picture."

Belinda gave me a pitying frown. "It's a picture that shows that whites and blacks are forced onto different sides of a racial barrier that keeps us apart. And it shows two kids trying to break down those barriers."

"It does?"

Belinda blew out her breath. Her eyelids sagged real low. "That's what Mrs. Took has been trying to tell you," she said.

"But what about your poems?" I asked. "Aren't they racist? I mean you write about black people."

"Merciful heaven," Belinda said in a perfect imitation of Mae. She expanded her arms in an all-encompassing gesture.

"Look at me," she said. "I'm black as a skillet, so I can write about being black. But if I wrote about whites, they'd string me up like they did that boy in Alabama."

I guess that made sense, but I didn't like the thought of anybody hurting Belinda.

"If your poems aren't racist, then what are they?" I asked.

"My poems are just *about* race, just like your pictures," Belinda said. "You can write and draw about race and racism without being racist."

That didn't make much sense. Weren't they the same thing?

"Then why are you trapped in the darkness of your people?" I asked. I never understood that part of her poem.

"We're all trapped in the darkness of our people," she said. "I'm trapped in my skin and you're trapped in yours. It's just a different kind of darkness, that's all."

I thought about that for a long time while Belinda yanked up a stray dandelion and began shredding its butter-colored petals like it had insulted her entire family. I tried to figure out what my darkness might be. If Damon had been a white guy, would I have kept the money?

An emptiness expanded in the pit of my stomach. If I was going to be honest, I had to admit that I would have run home and told my parents if it had been a white guy. I had even wondered if Damon might be a thug or a gangster—as if black men with money could only come by it illegally. Did that mean I was racist? Had I absorbed the darkness of my skin color, of white society, of my people? This must have been what Dwight had been explaining to Leroy.

I picked at the grass as the horror of what I had done sank into my soul like never before. How had I missed all of this when it was so obvious to other people? Maybe it was because Belinda and the other kids at school who weren't white had to deal with discrimination every day. I had grown-up blissfully unaware of it because it didn't affect me. But what I had done proved I was trapped in the darkness of my people without being able to see it for what it was.

"I don't like the darkness," I mumbled.

Belinda opened her mouth as if she meant to give me a thrashing. But she stopped, closed it, and dropped her gaze to her hands where the mangled dandelion sagged, pinched between her fingers. She dropped it as if suddenly disgusted by it.

"Me neither," she said.

The creek trickled past, and the breeze whispered through the still, bare branches of the birch trees. A few birds squabbled somewhere. I sat there wondering what a person did once he realized he was filled with a darkness that made him hurt other people. How did he make it right?

"I got expelled," Belinda said.

I glanced at her. It took me half a second to understand what she said.

"For what?"

"Not from here," she said with a roll of her big, sky-blue eyes. "From Mobile. I got in a lot of fights. That's why Mom sent me here to be with Grandma."

"Was it because of the darkness?" I asked.

Belinda surveyed me until I squirmed under her gaze.

"I guess it was," she said. "People got lots of darkness inside them—even kids."

That night, Mom and the pink-eyed devil became acquainted. It wasn't a long acquaintance, and it ended in violence with a lot of shrieking and stomping. Usually, Mom tried to keep as much distance as possible between her and any small furry creature, but this time she snapped. She lost it. I don't know if it's because the gerbil came flying out of her utensil drawer when she opened it or if the Force told her that demon of a gerbil tried to ruin her own son's life. But whatever it was, the Force was with her because, as she stomped after the tailless beast, her heel came down at just the right moment to catch the gerbil as it skidded into a corner. There was a crunch and a spattering of blood on the wall. Mom just stood there breathing like a marathon runner, too terrified to lift her foot. She must have remembered what happened last time she and a mouse tangled in the kitchen.

Thus ended the days of the pink-eyed monster gerbil who spent the last months of her life ostracized from the society of man and mouse. The Houdini of mice, the wrecker of fortunes, the tormentor of childhood died as she deserved. I tried to feel sorry for the gerbil, but I didn't try very hard. It seemed to me that God decided to cast me one tiny morsel of revenge for all I had suffered. Maybe now my luck would change for the better.

CHAPTER TWENTY-SIX
THE CONFESSION

I stared at the pile of cash on my bed. After I collected for my two paper routes that month, I had more than enough to cover the six hundred dollars I owed Mae. But my stomach soured, and I got weak in the knees every time I thought about giving her the money. I invented a million and one ways to do it without her knowing it was me. I could mail it to her. I could leave it on her porch some dark night. I could bake it in a cake. But, in the end, I couldn't do it that way.

My deformed brain had already created enough problems for me. I needed to make a clean breast of it sooner or later. I had to tell her face to face, but the mere thought turned my knees to jelly and my stomach into a boiling tar pit. Mae and Belinda were the only friends I had. I didn't want to lose them, but I couldn't keep Damon's money any longer. Mae needed it. She needed to know what I knew about Damon. I couldn't hide from my conscience any longer. Mae deserved the truth.

I waited until the day before Easter. Mae might not have been Christian, but I hoped she would be more willing to forgive me on a religious holiday. I excavated my glass jar from under the sycamore and counted out the bills. I had almost four thousand dollars. I figured I owed her at least a few hundred in interest. But I didn't go straight to Mae's House. I rode my bike to the park, sat on the bridge, and dangled my legs over the edge. The envelope filled with cash bulged in my pocket.

"I'm finally gonna do it, Damon," I said. "I'm going to do the right thing for once."

A breeze rustled through the trees, and I swear I heard a voice say, "Thank you." It didn't matter if the voice was real or not. That "thank you" whispered in the wind of Damon's death place carried me all the way to Mae's house and up onto her porch. My legs turned to wet spaghetti noodles, and my insides felt like an army of ants on the march.

The whole plan made a lot of sense in my head—until I stood before her door with an envelope full of money clutched in my hand. Then it seemed desperately stupid.

I raised my trembling hand to knock on the door. The air became thin. I couldn't breathe. I couldn't do it. I just couldn't. I turned to leave, but that "thank you" echoed in my mind. Damon was counting on me. I turned and faced the door again, swallowed, and knocked—softly at first, then louder. Once I started, I wanted to get it over with.

If getting there was hard, speaking to Mae was impossible. I stared up into her round face and bright eyes and wanted to melt into the floor. She cocked her head sideways.

"James?" she asked as her brow furrowed into neat little rows.

I tried to say something, but my tongue quit working. Mae backed away from the door and invited me in. I shuffled into her front room, casting a nervous glance at Damon's picture, while she closed the door. Then I handed her the envelope. She frowned and opened it.

Her eyes bulged. Her lips parted in surprise. Her brow folded in on itself, and she raised her gaze to stare at me. I shrank under her scrutiny. I swallowed.

"It's Damon's money," I croaked. "I'm the one that found his body. I took the wallet before I knew it was his—before I ever discovered his body." I whispered the words, but they hit the air like ice on a fire. Mae stumbled backward and fell into a chair. The money slipped to the floor and spread out like a green disease. She stared and stared and stared.

"I'm so sorry," I said. Then the words rushed out of me. "I would have given it to you months ago if it hadn't been for my stupid gerbil. He ate six hundred dollars, and I had to get a second paper route to earn the money, and then our car broke down, and I had to help pay for the repairs so we could buy groceries."

I stopped speaking because it didn't seem like Mae was listening.

"I never spent any of it," I whispered, "and I added a couple of hundred dollars in interest."

A horrible wriggling feeling swarmed over my entire body. I had said the words. I had returned the money, but somehow this didn't fix things the way it had in my imagination.

Tears slipped from Mae's eyes to roll down her cheeks. An expression of horror and disbelief froze on her face. I shuffled my feet and stuffed my hands into my pockets, searching for any sign of forgiveness on her smooth, dark-skinned face.

Her eyes bulged. Her lip lifted in a snarl. Her nostrils flared. I wanted to melt into the floor, to disappear.

Mae launched to her feet. She cocked back a meaty hand and slapped me across the face so hard I staggered into her side table.

The lamp flew to the floor with a crash as the pain of her hand burned my cheek like I had dropped it into a hot frying pan.

But the pain in my face was nothing to the agony that stabbed my chest as if she had rammed one of her knitting needles straight through my heart. Mae and Belinda were the only friends I had, except for Damon's ghost.

"Get out!" she screamed. "Get out!"

I staggered toward the door. Shocked. Frightened. Confused.

"I never should have expected anything else from a white boy," she growled. "Get out of my house and never come back."

The harsh words chased me out the door and all the way to Damon's bridge where I crumpled into a heap and wept. I deserved what I got, but that didn't make me feel any better. The welt from her slap burned on my cheek. Mae was probably on the phone with the police that very moment. I would spend Easter in jail— which is where I belonged. What had I expected her to do? Give me a big, wet kiss?

I whirled at the sound of something scratching across the bridge. The black and white dog padded up and pushed his wet nose against my cheek. I reached up to shove him away, but I remembered what the old man from my paper route had told me. Friends were hard to come by, even friends that smelled like a dirty dog.

I slumped on the bridge with my arm around the dog. The darkness swallowed the light and the world became as blank and empty as my heart. The dog followed me home until I rolled my bike onto the grass. He stopped and wagged his tail.

"Come on," I said. He didn't seem to have an owner, and I figured he could stay with us. I wanted him to stay with me. I needed him to stay. He barked, wagged his tail, and trotted away. I watched him go, wondering where he went at night and how he always seemed to find me at the worst moments of my life.

No police cars with blue flashing lights waited for me, so I slipped into my room—like the rat I had become. Mom had already gone to work. Dad was working on some school project in his room, so it was easy to hide. I curled up in the corner in the gloom, wishing I could escape the darkness inside, while I waited for the police to barge through the door and drag me away to jail.

CHAPTER TWENTY-SEVEN
THE ULTIMATUM

The police hadn't come to arrest me by Sunday morning, so I got up to deliver my papers. I grabbed a handful of Easter candy and headed across the front lawn. Something swaying from the branches of the big sycamore tree caught my attention. The frail light of morning still struggled to make its way into the world, so I couldn't tell what it was from a distance.

I thought it might be an opossum. When I got closer, I found someone had left an Easter gift for me. A bunny was hanging from the lowest branch with a noose tied around its neck. Clint, who was heading out for his morning route, strode right up to it. I didn't want to get anywhere near the rabbit, but he reached up and pulled something off of it, examined it, and turned to me with a scowl. The bunny dangled behind him, stiff in death.

Clint held the piece of paper out. I pulled it from his hand and read it. "Zero, stay away from the Oreo."

"You understand what that means?" he questioned.

I blinked at him and shook my head. I couldn't tell him. I didn't know how. Besides, I knew what he would say. He would tell me to fight them, but I had tried that. This was a lot more complicated than simple bullying. No fight was going to solve it. I found myself all tangled up in histories I knew nothing about, which meant I didn't have any idea how to untangle myself.

He gave me that narrow-eyed, suspicious stare that made

133

me want to blurt it all out. I knew he didn't believe me. But he shrugged and yanked the bunny down.

"I'm gonna tell Dad," he said.

I suppose he was thinking about Oscar's dad and the eggs he threw at us. But I couldn't let him tell Dad. Not now.

I grabbed his arm. "Don't," I said. "I'll tell them."

I figured Mom and Dad were gonna have enough to deal with when the police came to arrest me. Clint glared at me.

"What are you up to?" he demanded. "Did you hang this here?"

"No," I blurted. The very idea was insulting.

He studied me. "I told you to fight 'em," he said. "If someone's after you, you better fight 'em before this gets worse."

"I will," I said as I grabbed the stiff rabbit from his hands.

I hid it by the creek on the way to my paper route. I would come back and give it a proper burial. This problem wasn't going to go away. Fists and fighting were no use because I couldn't fight every kid at school, and I sure as heck couldn't fight the adults.

The police hadn't come for me by Monday morning either, so I acted like I wasn't on their most wanted list and snuck away to school. Belinda wouldn't talk to me, and when Mr. Sentury decided to sacrifice somebody on an Aztec altar, I couldn't take it. I didn't want to think about Michael Donald being murdered because of someone's belief or about Dwight and the Vietnam War.

What if Damon had been killed for some equally stupid reason? When Mr. Sentury had a boy draped over his desk with an eraser held in one hand like a knife, I raised my hand and asked to be excused to go to the restroom.

There was something wrong about killing someone because they were from a different group, but it seemed worse when it was done in the name of some religion. I attended church every week, and, even though people didn't always act the way they said they believed, I didn't think religion should be used to justify murder.

After class, I found another note in my locker. It read: "Eternal vigilance is the price of freedom. All whites should give the blacks what they deserve." Someone had drawn a hangman's scaffold with a stick figure hanging from it. I wanted to scream and punch someone, anyone, but that would only get me into more trouble. I slammed my fist into the locker instead. This time, I didn't have to punch it twice to leave my knuckle prints.

In art class, I started on a new drawing after I finished the watercolor painting Mrs. Took had assigned. I knew the painting was awful because I didn't understand colors, and I wanted to draw something else—something that had bothered me for a long time. It was like it itched at my fingers until I put pencil to paper.

My pencil scratched the drawing paper as I outlined the log where I found Damon's body. Then I sketched in the turtles before I drew in the shape of his body curled up against the log. For some reason, this picture seemed to be the easiest one I'd ever drawn. It was as if Damon had been living in my fingers, waiting for them to bring him back to life.

But I couldn't do that. I didn't know enough about his life and, to me, he had always been dead. All I could do was draw his death— to bring him back into the world as a pile of clothes. My fingers seemed to know what to do. I had most of it sketched by the end of class when Mrs. Took loomed up behind me.

I snatched the picture off the desk and peered up at her, hoping against hope she hadn't seen what I had been drawing. But the crease between her brows didn't give me much reason to hope. Her gaze shifted to my drawing, and the frown deepened.

"Please remain after class," she said.

After everyone else left, and I stood fidgeting by her desk, looking everywhere but at her. She sat down and glared up at me.

"Explain," she said.

For such a small person, she sure could be intimidating.

I shrugged. "I'm not very good at painting. I can't get the colors right."

"That's not what I mean."

She snapped her fingers and held out her hand.

I swallowed.

"Let me see it," she said.

I shrugged off my backpack and retrieved the drawing.

She studied it for a long time. "Do you remember when I told you that art was a window onto the artist's soul?"

I nodded.

"Your drawings have become progressively darker," she said. "You started out with sadness and race, and now you have drawn death. Why?"

I stood there, pinching my lips tight, trying to figure out how to get out of this.

She frowned and glanced down at the picture again. "Is this real? Have you really seen this?"

I swallowed. Should I tell her? Could I? My hands grew cold, and I started to sweat. But something in my face betrayed me.

Mrs. Took's frown deepened. "I see," she said. "When?"

"Beginning of the summer."

"Where?"

"In the park by my house."

"Have you told your parents?"

I shook my head and pinched my lips tight again.

Mrs. Took sucked in a deep breath. "Is this the man who was found in Stillwater Creek?"

My eyes went wide, and the Grand Canyon opened in the pit of my stomach. This time, I was up to my eyeballs in doo-doo. I nodded. I glanced at the door thinking now might be a good time to make a break for it.

"Do you have any idea how serious this is?"

I faced her again and nodded.

"Do the police know you found him?"

I shook my head.

Mrs. Took sat back, blew out her air and shook her head. "I'll give you until tomorrow to tell your parents," she said. "Then I'm calling them."

"What?" I shouted.

I wanted to protest the injustice of it. I had already made things right with Mae—even if she did hate me. If she hadn't called the police, I couldn't see why anyone else had a right to worry about it, and why I needed to tell my parents anything. They could go on living in happy ignorance that they had raised a brain-damaged knucklehead for a son.

But Mrs. Took withered me with a glance. "You are swimming in deep waters way over your head, James. Of all of my students, I would expect you to see this."

CHAPTER TWENTY-EIGHT
FEATHERED FRIENDS

How do you explain to your parents that you have failed them in everything they've tried to teach you? That you've been dodging the police for months? That you're guilty of a dozen crimes? That just about every black kid and white kid in school wanted to beat you to a pulp?

Well, I couldn't tell them. Not yet, so I rushed off to deliver my evening papers. Maybe some kind of divine inspiration would strike me. Or a ray of sunlight would pierce my thick skull and repair my damaged brain. Maybe Obi-Wan Kenobi would appear and use the Force to drag me away from the Dark Side that waited to gobble me up alive, to save me from the darkness of my people, from the darkness in my own heart.

Nothing magical happened. In fact, nothing at all happened until I reached the place on my route where the trees came in, close and wild. It was the swampy area where the little stream that passed Mae's house slowed down and lost itself amid the grasses and thorns. To me, it had always been a lonely place, a place to hurry through.

As my defective brain wrestled to work out what to say to my parents, a scream echoed through the trees, ricocheting in every direction. I slammed on the brakes and skidded to a stop in a cloud of dust.

Someone shouted. Boys laughed. A dog barked. I turned toward the voices as my heart picked up the pace of its nervous beating. Someone screamed again. My mind zoomed into focus. I recognized that scream.

I spun my bike around and raced toward the voices and the barking. A narrow trail—too narrow for a bike—cut into the woods. I jumped off and sprinted into the brush. Branches reached out to pluck at my clothes and pinch my face. Water splashed around my feet. The voices grew louder. Then I crashed into a clearing and skidded to a stop.

The fading light of day slanted through the trees and rested on Belinda, who struggled against the dark figures in hooded sweatshirts tying a gag over her mouth. The black and white dog was already tied to a tree, where it barked and lunged against the rope. I froze in stunned horror. My mind raced to the boy killed in Alabama. Before I thought about what I was doing, I found myself running toward her, yelling at the top of my lungs.

"Leave her alone!"

More than a dozen hooded figures straightened and turned towards me, looming in the fading light like ghouls on the prowl. I realized I had raced right into a circle of hooded figures. They weren't wearing hoods like the clan. Just dark sweatshirts with the hoods pulled up. The flames of a bonfire licked up the sides of a crudely made cross.

"Well, if it isn't the Zero," someone said.

I recognized the voice.

"Let her go, Oscar," I demanded.

"I don't think so," Oscar said. "But now, we don't have to go looking for you. Get him!" he yelled.

Before I could do more than give one feeble swing at the first kid that barreled into me, I was on the bottom of a pile that threatened to crush my ribs. By the time they had me tied up and leaned against the tree beside Belinda, I had nearly suffocated. My mind raced as fast as my heart.

Oscar paced in front of us like Mr. Sentury did when he was getting ready to lead us in another execution. Oscar's goons stood in a menacing semi-circle around us.

I wanted to be brave, but my imagination snapped its leash as terrifying images of Damon and Michael being murdered and

Dwight being blown up chased each other around in my brain. I trembled. Sweat ran down my back and dripped into my eyes. Maybe Belinda and I would end up in the creek, crumpled in death against Damon's log.

"We have tried and convicted Mr. Zero and Miss Oreo," Oscar said in his best lawyer voice, "for treason against their own color. Now they will have to pay for their crimes."

I exchanged a nervous glance with Belinda. Her eyes were wide, and her eyebrows rode high on her forehead. Her nostrils flared like a wild horse. I half-expected her to snap the ropes that bound her and leap up like an African Wonder Woman. But she didn't. And what the heck was a crime against my color? I had never heard of such a thing.

"What are you talking about?" I yelled.

Oscar ignored me and gestured to one of the hooded figures who produced a long rope with a big noose tied on one end. He tossed the noose over a low-lying tree branch and secured the loose end to a tree. Another kid produced a doll with half its face painted black and the other half painted white. He slipped the noose around the doll's neck and jerked it tight. The doll swung back and forth as the shadows deepened and the flickering light of the fire jumped across its face.

"Since both of you don't like the color of your skin," Oscar said, "we have decided to change it for you."

Belinda rubbed her head against the tree trying to wiggle the gag free. It slipped from her mouth.

"You're all a bunch of cowards!" she yelled. "You won't get away with this!"

Oscar stopped pacing. "Shut up," he said. "If you weren't such a big mouth gutter monkey, we wouldn't be here."

A couple of boys turned their heads to look at each other as if they didn't like what Oscar said.

"The police will find out," I said. "You're all going to jail."

Oscar shrugged. "We aren't doing anything illegal. And this is for your own good. You two have to learn your place." He gestured to the pack of hooded figures. "Bring out the honey."

I thought I heard him wrong. Boiling oil, I would have understood. But honey? What could he want with honey? Was he going to make us eat it until we collapsed into some kind of sugar coma? Had he killed rabbits and stuffed them in the honey the way the Egyptians did babies? Two boys stomped up, each carrying a big gallon-jar of honey. They twisted the lids off and dumped the honey over our heads without ceremony.

I jerked to get out of the way, but another boy grabbed me and held me. The honey was smooth and cool. It smelled good and tasted better, but it got into my eyes when I blinked. My eyelashes stuck together. The world became a blurry prism in which everything twisted and wavered. But I could make out the shapes of more boys stepping forward carrying bulging sacks.

They upended the sacks and shook the contents over our heads. Black feathers floated down around me, lifting on my breath as I blew out my air. One flew right up my nose, and I sneezed. People started laughing.

I tried to see what happened to Belinda. Through my blurry, black-feathered vision, I saw that she had been covered in white feathers.

Applause rang out. People hooted and hollered.

"Behold Zero and Oreo," Oscar intoned. "They finally look like they should."

Boys laughed. Burning anger rose in my belly, filling me with indignation as hot as the bonfire.

"You're a jerk and a coward, Oscar!" I yelled. "You're nothing but a racist pig!" Once I got started, I couldn't stop. "Everyone here knows," I continued, "the only reason you don't like black people is because your dad is an ignorant bigot and because you know most of those black folks are ten times the man you'll ever be." I was thinking of Dwight and Mae and Damon and Belinda.

Oscar stomped up and punched me right in the nose. Pain lanced across my face. My eyes stung. I blinked at the tears that rose up to blind me. The metallic taste of blood mingled with the sweetness of honey on my tongue. I couldn't help but think of the story Mr. Sentury told us about the mummified baby hair in the honey. I didn't want that in my mouth. I spat on the ground.

"You wouldn't do that if we could fight back," I said. "You're a coward!"

I didn't know where all this defiance was coming from. I guess

WALLS OF GLASS

I couldn't take it anymore. Most of the year I had spent trying to avoid them, trying to keep from being a target. But what had that accomplished? They came after me anyway. I struggled against the knots on my wrists. They seemed to loosen a little.

"Let's do it," Oscar said. "Let's give this little Zero a real scare."

The hollering and clapping stuttered to silence.

"What do you mean?" one of the other boys asked.

"Let's stretch his wimpy neck just a bit," Oscar said. "Let him see what it feels like to be a traitor."

CHAPTER TWENTY-NINE
THE NOOSE

An eerie quiet settled over the clearing. The fire popped. Frogs called to each other.

"We agreed not to hurt them," someone else said.

"I'm not gonna hurt him," Oscar said. "Just scare him." Oscar yanked the doll from the noose and pulled it wider. "Bring him here," he demanded.

No one moved.

"Just bring him here!" Oscar yelled.

Two boys stepped forward, untied my feet, and dragged me toward the noose. My hands were still bound behind my back, but the cords were coming loose.

"Stop it!" Belinda screamed. "Stop it!"

I thought Belinda was so tough she never felt afraid, but the terror in her voice made the blood run cold in my veins. Oscar slipped the noose over my head and pulled the rope tight so that my tiptoes barely touched the ground. I struggled to breathe, trying to stand as tall as I could. If the noose pulled any tighter, I wouldn't be able to breathe at all.

Oscar tied the rope to the tree again and turned to face the half circle of silent boys with a triumphant smile. A tall boy jumped forward and shoved Oscar away from the tree.

"No way," he said. "We're not doing this." He bent to untie the rope.

WALLS OF GLASS

Oscar scrambled to his feet and shoved the boy back. "Get out of my way, Leroy."

"Dude," Leroy said, "you can't do something like this. Didn't you hear what happened in Alabama?"

"This was *your* idea," Oscar said. "You wanted to scare them, especially the little Oreo. Now get out of my way so I can scare them."

"Not. Like. This," Leroy said. He pulled his hood back and shook his head. His afro stood out everywhere. His face glistened in the flickering light of the fire, but his eyes were huge and white. "My great granddad was lynched," he said. "I won't let you do it."

Oscar jumped on Leroy with a savage cry. "You stupid knuckle dragger," he screamed.

"White trash," Leroy hollered.

As Oscar and Leroy pummeled each other, they knocked into me. The rope jerked tight around my throat, burning like fire. I gave a strangled cry as pandemonium erupted all around me. I danced under the rope seeking firm footing with my tiptoes, jerking at the ropes that still bound my hands. My lungs burned. My chest contracted in a spasmodic attempt to find air. I scrambled on the slippery leaves on tiptoe as I swung back and forth. In my panic, I couldn't get the ground under me to hold still. It kept moving and swaying and slipping away.

The edges of my vision began to blur. I was going to die. I was actually going to die by hanging while the boys fought all around me, oblivious to the fact that they were killing me. I thought of my parents and wondered if they would hold a candlelight vigil for me. Would anybody come to remember a white kid who had died by accident?

The rope jerked loose from the tree, and I slammed to the ground. The noose loosened enough to allow a little air into my lungs. I choked and gasped, sucking in the sweet air. It smelled of honey and smoke and earth and sweat and fear, but it was the sweetest thing I had ever tasted.

Then I was crying and choking as I struggled against the rope on my wrists. Good thing these guys weren't Boy Scouts. Their knots weren't much good. I pulled and twisted until one hand slipped free. By some magic, it came undone.

143

I yanked the noose from my neck and sucked in the beautiful, sweet air, trying not to sob out loud. I spun to find Belinda struggling against her ropes—so covered in white feathers that her upper body looked like a ghost floating in the darkness.

As the boys brawled all around the clearing, I rushed to Belinda and untied her hands and legs.

"Get out of here," I choked.

She grabbed my hand to drag me after her, but I pulled my hand free.

"I'll keep them from coming after you," I said.

Belinda stared at me with wide frightened eyes. "Come on," she pleaded.

"No. They'll catch us." I turned toward the fire, but Belinda caught my hand again. Her gaze searched my face. I must have looked stupid all covered in dirty honey, black chicken feathers, and old leaves.

"Thank you," she said, "for being my friend."

I nodded, pulling my hand free. I dashed to the fire, selected two big burning sticks, and jerked them free. Gesturing for Belinda to run, I followed her toward the trail whose opening was visible as a darker stain against the blackness of the trees. The firebrands blew out as we ran and became ghostly red, spitting sparks that flared in the night before they fell to the damp ground and died.

"They're getting away," someone shouted.

Others took up the cry, and soon the mob was sprinting after us. I didn't have time to ponder the weirdness of this whole mess. One second, both black and white were united in their hatred of us. The next they were pounding on each other, screaming racial slurs. And then they were united again.

"Run!" I yelled. "Get out of here!"

"Come on," Belinda said.

"Get going," I replied.

Belinda hesitated. The whites of her eyes shone as white as the feathers that clung to her head and upper body.

"Go!" I yelled.

Desperation choked me. If I didn't get her out of there, things would get a lot worse. But she finally ran, a ghostly shadow bobbing into the darkness until she disappeared into the trees.

WALLS OF GLASS

I faced the mob, knowing it was suicide. But, if I could keep them from getting a hold of Belinda again, that was all that mattered. As they approached, I swung the firebrands like swords. Red sparks sizzled through the darkness like evil, little fireflies.

"Stay away from me!" I screamed.

"Now you're gonna get it," Oscar said.

Somebody lunged when a white streak flashed out of the darkness to knock him aside. The dog snarled, its hackles raised as it positioned itself between me and the boys. It trailed a length of frayed rope.

I whirled and ran. The dog barked and snarled, but it couldn't keep all the boys at bay. A rock slammed into my back, and I spun to face them brandishing the glowing sticks.

One boy was so close he couldn't stop before I hit him with the brand. He shrieked like a pig and fell back. They all paused. Oscar lunged in, but I clocked him upside the head.

More crashing sounded in the bushes all around me. I backed up on the narrow trail, trying to keep them from getting behind me. Someone yelled, and they all rushed me with a roar. I hit a couple of them with the firebrands, but they were like an army of ants swarming in for the kill. Soon, I was on the ground under the crushing weight of a pile of boys trying to punch me and kick me to kingdom come.

If they hadn't tried to do it all at once they would have done a better job. In the darkness, they hit and kicked each other a lot more than they did me. The dog barked and growled. Someone cried out in pain.

I don't know how long I lay there curled up in a ball, trying to protect my head and chest, before the shrill scream of sirens ripped through the darkness. The roar of the mob changed pitch, and soon they were scrambling to get away from me. Someone gave me one last parting kick, and I was alone in the darkness—alone with the pain. This didn't bother me as much as I thought it would. At least the pain told me I was alive.

I crawled over to the nearest tree and tried to sit up. Fire lanced through my side. My head felt like someone had been tapping on it with a sledgehammer. I swallowed the blood and bile in my throat and tried to breathe. I curled up against the tree in the darkness and, trying to understand, trying to make sense of a messed-up world where black and white were opposites that weren't supposed to mix. The dog whined and licked at my face. I tried to focus through the blur of pain and honey that stuck to my eyelids.

"Thanks pal," I mumbled and stroked his matted fur.

Booted feet pounded the ground. Beams of light danced in the darkness. Soon, large hands were helping me lie down. Policemen began asking me all kinds of questions. How do you explain that you were attacked by a mob of kids who didn't even follow their own rules when your head was splitting open and your ribs were scraping together?

I wondered what the policemen thought of me, lying there covered in black feathers and honey like some Halloween costume gone terribly wrong.

CHAPTER THIRTY
THE SHATTERING

Clint was not happy about doing my paper routes for a few days while I lounged on the couch, trying not to move. The newspaper headlines read, "Hate Crime Comes to Stillwater." They got the story more or less right, but they wrote my name as Jim—which added insult to injury. I wanted to call them to make them change it, but Mom wouldn't let me. Oscar, Leroy, and their gangs found themselves in the juvenile detention system. I had to give a police statement about the hate crime, but otherwise I tried to forget about it.

True to her word, Mrs. Took called and told my parents about Damon. The conversation that followed was the worst conversation I ever had with my parents. They were beside themselves. It must have been quite a shock to learn they had raised the most foolish kid in the entire western half of the United States. I don't think they've gotten over it yet.

My dad visited Mae to apologize and to ask her what she wanted him to do. He was ready to report me to the police if Mae wanted him to. Can you imagine that? My own father was willing to sell me out. But Mae, good old Mae, came to my rescue again.

"I'd rather just let this whole thing die down and go away," she told him. "Besides he saved my granddaughter."

Well, that was a relief because Mae had it in her power to throw me into the slammer for a long time. And I deserved it.

Mrs. Spencer and Jeremy came over to gloat, even after what they did to us. Some people have no shame. Mrs. Spencer didn't even bring any cookies or anything. I think she wanted to see how beat up I was. She shook her head and clicked her tongue.

"This is what comes from letting your children run wild and associate with colored folks," she said.

At the word "colored," Mom grabbed Mrs. Spencer's arm and propelled her toward the door.

"You can take your bigotry elsewhere," Mom said and slammed the door in their faces.

Mom spun to stare at me. Her nostrils flared, and I thought she might explode. Then a slow smile spread over her face.

"That felt good," she said. "Really good."

I wanted to jump up and down and cheer. Or maybe give Mom a big, wet kiss, but I wasn't sure how Mom would respond, and my ribs hurt too much.

The Spencers' visit made me think of mice and gerbils. I wondered if the Spencers saw me the same way I saw the pink-eyed devil gerbil—annoying, a little frightening, maybe even dangerous. When the gerbil got in the way of my plans and hopes and dreams, I tried to crush her. The stupid animal didn't understand the rules about money. To her, it was a material for making a warm nest.

Maybe that was why both the white and black kids picked on me. Since I didn't understand the rules, I had disrupted them—thrown them all out of whack. They had been trying to put me back into the comfortable categories they created for me—to stick me behind the walls of glass where I could see the other categories, but not interfere with them.

It didn't work. Walls of glass are brittle and easily broken. Belinda and I chipped tiny little cracks that revealed their hypocrisy, and the glass walls came crashing down. Those who built them and maintained them attacked us for it, but it didn't matter. People like Oscar, and Leroy, and the Spencers were just going to rebuild them. I don't think they knew how to live without them. Walls of glass gave them the illusion of control. The masquerade that they were special. That they mattered more than everybody else.

WALLS OF GLASS

A couple of days later, Mae and Belinda came to see me.

"Hey," I said as Mom let them in. My insides wiggled around, and my face burned with shame. I sat up straighter, preparing to hear the worst.

Belinda smiled. "You all right?" she asked.

"Yeah. How about you?"

She shrugged. "I've had worse."

We both grinned.

"I'll never get the smell of honey out of my hair though," she said.

Mae settled her bulk into the chair beside me while Mom went to get them some refreshments. Mae rested her dimpled hand on my arm. The contrast of her dark skin against my white skin made me think of my glass wall drawing. Light and shadow. Black and white.

It struck me then that I had been looking at things the wrong way. I thought it had all been about the color of our skin, but the color on the outside had nothing to do with it. It was the darkness on the inside that made people do bad things. Skin color was just an excuse. That was what Belinda had been writing about in her poem. I didn't understand where that darkness came from, but the thought bothered me. How do you fight the darkness inside when you can't even see it or give it a name?

Mae pulled a piece of paper and a photo out of her handbag.

"I received this letter in the mail yesterday," she said. "I think you should read it."

I glanced at Belinda as her face settled into a sad frown. But she nodded encouragement. I took the paper and read aloud.

"Dear Mrs. Wiggins,

"I saw the obituary for your late husband in the paper. I recognized his kind face. I want you to know that we are alive today because of his sacrifice. He was the only man brave enough to jump into the flash flood to pull my baby and me from our car. He had just handed my little girl up to a bystander on the street when the branch he clung to snapped, and he was swept away in the torrent. We couldn't do anything to save him. I am so sorry for your loss and so grateful that he sacrificed his life to save ours. I do not know what comfort this might give you in your grief. But I wanted you to know that he will live on in our memories and in the life of my little girl.

Yours in gratitude,
Mable Peterson"

I held up the photo. A white woman held a chubby, blonde girl in her arms. I swallowed the lump in my throat and blinked at the sudden stinging in my eyes. What could I say? Damon hadn't been murdered. Damon was a hero.

Mom stood in the doorway with a tray in her hands and an expression of shock on her face. Mae dabbed at her eyes with a handkerchief, and Belinda sniffled.

Mae cleared her throat. "James," she said, "I have lived my entire life fighting for equality and civil rights for black people. In all that time, I never once confronted the racism that lurked in my own heart until the day you told me what you had done."

I looked away. She reached a hand to my chin and pulled it around until I was facing her again.

"My heart was so bitter," she said. "I hated you."

I stiffened. Here it came. She was going to give me the tongue lashing I deserved. It's never easy to hear that someone hates you, but when it comes from one of the only two friends you have, it really tears at your insides. Mae pinched her lips tight, and I blinked at the tears that welled up in my eyes.

"Then," she continued, "when I received this letter and learned that my own sweet Damon had died to save a white woman—well, I've never been so ashamed. He didn't just talk about loving our neighbors. He died for it. What you did was wrong, but what I did was also wrong. It has taken me some time to learn to forgive you."

I nodded because I understood. I could only imagine how she had felt. I don't know if I would have been able to forgive someone who had done what I had.

"Now, will you forgive me?" she asked.

I sat in stunned silence. I had wronged this woman in the worst possible way, and here she was asking *me* for forgiveness. I had acted like a racist, and she was asking *me* for forgiveness.

I shook my head to contradict her. When shock registered on her face, I realized that she thought I was saying I wouldn't forgive her. I blurted out a desperate explanation.

"I deserved it," I said. "After what I did, you should lock me up for the rest of my life."

Now Mae smiled a big, toothy grin. "I've never met a boy with such a nose for trouble," she said. "You can't even accept an apology without diving right into it."

Well, she was right. But at least I had found the courage to do the right thing the first time around. Maybe there was hope for me after all.

Mom set the tray on the coffee table and sat beside me. She took my hand. Tears glistened in her eyes.

Mae shook her head back and forth. "Sometimes," she said, "I'm afraid that everything we suffered has been wasted. Sometimes I worry that my grandchildren won't understand what it was like. And I worry that whites and blacks alike won't ever learn to let each other be and learn to celebrate our differences."

Then Mae smiled at me again. "And now I look at you and Belinda, and I see there's reason to hope."

I wiggled off the couch, trying not to wince too much from the pain in my ribs. I gave Mae a big hug, hoping she wouldn't see the tears in my eyes. She was round and soft and smelled of coconut and cinnamon.

I shook hands with Belinda because . . .well, she's a girl.

It was the year I killed the cardinal and the year I met Damon Wiggins at Stillwater Creek. It was the year I tangled with the Dark Side that lurked in my own soul and won a small victory. It was the year I searched for an Obi-Wan Kenobi only to find that he was me. Okay, not quite, but almost.

No matter how hard I tried, I found myself entangled in struggles that had been going on for centuries before I was born. By trying to avoid the galactic battles, I made sure they found me. I awakened the darkness that sleeps in all of us by trying to act like it didn't exist or like I could hide from it. But I broke through the walls of glass, and I wasn't going to be controlled by those who built them ever again. Maybe the galactic battles were worth fighting—even when you're the new kid in town.

ABOUT J.W. ELLIOT

J.W. Elliot is a professional historian, martial artist, canoer, bow builder, knife maker, woodturner, and rock climber. He has a Ph.D. in Latin American and World History. He has lived in Idaho, Oklahoma, Brazil, Arizona, Portugal, and Massachusetts. He writes non-fiction works of history about the Inquisition, Columbus, and pirates. J.W. Elliot loves to travel and challenge himself in the outdoors.

Connect with J.W. Elliot online at:
www.jwelliot.com/contact-us

Archer of the Heathland
Prequel: *Intrigue*
Book I: *Deliverance*
Book II: *Betrayal*
Book III: *Vengeance*
Book IV: *Chronicles*
Book V: *Windemere*
Book VI: *Renegade*

The Miserable Life of Bernie LeBaron
Somewhere in the Mist
Walls of Glass

If you have enjoyed this book, please consider leaving an honest review on Amazon and sharing on your social media sites.

Please sign up for my newsletter where you can get a free short story and more free content at: **www.jwelliot.com**

Thanks for your support!

J.W. Elliot

Made in the USA
Middletown, DE
31 July 2020

14060685R00097